實用大學英語翻譯手冊

編著 ◎ 朱豔、王宏宇

Preface——前言

　　2016年上半年，據媒體報道，編者所在城市中心某條路上新立了一些很洋氣的中英文路牌，但有市民發現上面的英文有點別扭——"NIDDLE RING ROAD"。"這裡應該是'MIDDLE'吧？哪個外國人看得懂'NIDDLE'？"更有市民指出，即使拼寫沒有錯誤，將"中環路"譯爲"MIDDLE RING"也容易讓外國人產生誤解，還不如直接用漢語拼音"ZHONGHUAN ROAD"。也有市民建議把"中環路"翻譯爲"MID-RING ROAD"更顯正規。

　　一個粗心錯誤引出的討論，在當下中國卻並非孤例，相關報道屢屢見諸報端網路，被戲稱爲"神翻譯"。許多"神翻譯"滑稽程度遠超上述案例，更有不少是發生在具有相當影響力的大中城市，不能不說是對中國開放形象和城市文化形象的一種傷害。

　　這些問題產生的原因，主要在於相關人員的責任心不夠和水平不高。此外，新詞熱詞頻出、相關規範缺失也不容忽視。從"神翻譯"創作者身份分析，絕大部分應該受過高等教育，因此也暴露出高校英語教育存在的一些問題。作爲大學英語教師，我們認爲自己有責任在這方面做一些基礎性工作。一方面，這是大學英語教學的本質目標，另一方面，也切合了當前社會生活的現實需求。

　　在20多年的大學英語教學中，編者深深感覺到，大學生英語能力不強，詞彙是關鍵，專有詞、特殊詞是難點，學生常常無法將翻譯考試、求職及日常生活中涉及的一些漢語術語正確譯出。此外，學生對常用標識語、習慣表達法、相關翻譯規範也很不熟悉。此種情況不僅對學生的學業成績及求職就業產生影響，對跨文化交際和文化傳播也極爲不利。如果這方面的訓練不夠，學生在將來走向社會時，難免重犯上述滑稽的翻譯錯誤。

學生詞彙量不足，特別是對專有詞語把握不準，對西方文化認知欠缺，不熟悉翻譯規範，既與部分學生努力程度不夠有關，也與缺乏方便實用的工具書有關。基於此，我們希望編寫一本方便實用的大學英語翻譯手冊，既滿足教學工作的需要，也給社會各界有相關需求的人士提供一些參考。

在編纂本書的過程中，我們遵循幾個原則：第一，針對性。爲提高本書的針對性，我們突出需求導向。一是我們在長期翻譯教學過程中瞭解到的學生的不足之處、需求以及他們的關注點和興趣點；二是社會需求，包括常用詞語、易錯詞語、新詞熱詞、標識語等。按照需求分析安排相應章節及詞語。第二，準確性。編寫本書時我們盡可能參考權威書籍及權威媒體，針對部分新詞、熱詞、專有詞語，通過詞法分析，根據不同文化習俗和慣例給出參考翻譯方案。第三，再生性。本書不滿足於提供現成翻譯方案，更嘗試傳遞翻譯原則及表達規律，希望提高讀者再創造能力和面對新問題的應對能力。

全書涉及八部分的內容：第一單元——學校教育；第二單元——公共標識語；第三單元——烹飪及菜名；第四單元——傳統節日及習俗；第五單元——體育運動；第六單元——旅遊景點；第七單元——證書及職位；第八單元——熱詞、新詞、高頻詞。讀者可以根據需要查閱相關部分內容，也可以對各部分內容進行模仿學習。

編者

目 录

第一單元 學校教育 ……………………………………（1）
一、學校名稱參考翻譯方式 ………………………………（1）
二、各級各類學校名稱翻譯 ………………………………（5）
三、中國主要大學名稱翻譯 ………………………………（10）
四、學位名稱翻譯 …………………………………………（20）
五、學科及專業名稱翻譯 …………………………………（22）
六、教育常用語翻譯 ………………………………………（35）

第二單元 公共標識語 ……………………………………（40）
一、公共標識語的特點及表現形式 ………………………（40）
二、公共標識語常用的幾種英譯方式 ……………………（42）
三、常見公共標識語翻譯 …………………………………（45）

第三單元 烹飪及菜名 ……………………………………（62）
一、中國菜的分類 …………………………………………（63）
二、常用烹飪方法及調料翻譯 ……………………………（65）
三、菜名翻譯的幾種方法 …………………………………（67）
四、常見中餐菜名翻譯 ……………………………………（70）

第四單元 傳統節日及習俗 ………………………………（79）
一、中國主要傳統節日及習俗翻譯 ………………………（80）

二、中國二十四節氣翻譯 …………………………………………（91）

三、西方主要傳統節日及習俗翻譯 ………………………………（92）

第五單元　體育運動 ……………………………………………（102）

一、體育英語詞彙的構成 …………………………………………（102）

二、體育運動一般用語翻譯 ………………………………………（104）

三、世界大型體育運動會翻譯 ……………………………………（107）

四、國內外專項體育組織名稱翻譯 ………………………………（112）

五、世界主要體育賽事名稱翻譯 …………………………………（115）

六、熱門體育項目相關表達翻譯 …………………………………（117）

第六單元　旅遊景點 ……………………………………………（140）

一、旅遊景點翻譯的幾種方法 ……………………………………（140）

二、國內著名旅遊景點翻譯 ………………………………………（143）

三、旅遊相關表達翻譯 ……………………………………………（162）

四、世界著名旅遊景點翻譯 ………………………………………（166）

第七單元　證書及職位 …………………………………………（173）

一、證書的特點及翻譯常用句式 …………………………………（173）

二、證書翻譯範例 …………………………………………………（174）

三、考試及比賽名稱翻譯 …………………………………………（176）

四、職位名稱翻譯 …………………………………………………（179）

第八單元　熱詞、新詞、高頻詞 ………………………………（189）

一、政治類詞語翻譯 ………………………………………………（189）

二、法制類詞語翻譯 ………………………………………………（195）

三、環保類詞語翻譯 ………………………………………………（198）

四、社會民生類詞語翻譯 …………………………………………（202）

五、文教類詞語翻譯 ································（208）
　　六、網路流行語翻譯 ································（212）
參考文獻 ································（215）

第一單元
學校教育

　　學校教育是整個教育階段的關鍵。學校教育一般包括初等教育、中等教育和高等教育，包含幼兒園、小學、中學及大學幾個階段。學校教育是一個人一生中所受教育最重要的組成部分，決定着個人社會化的水平和性質。

　　作爲文化教育機構，學校教育及相關術語翻譯在規範性和準確性上的要求應該更高。近年來，高等院校在相關領域做得相對規範。但隨著國內中小學甚至幼兒園對外交往的需求逐漸增大，英文翻譯尤其是校名翻譯也暴露出了許多不規範、不準確的問題。

　　大學生在申請國外高校深造或求職時常常需要填寫中英文個人簡歷。能夠用英文比較準確填寫學校、專業、課程、學位等信息，是當今大學生必須具備的能力。

　　本單元簡單介紹學校名稱參考翻譯方式、各級各類學校名稱、中國主要高校名稱、學位名稱、學科和專業名稱以及教育相關術語的翻譯，供大學生和其他有需要的人士參考。

一、學校名稱參考翻譯方式

　　目前有關各類學校名稱翻譯很混亂 ，英式英語、美式英語甚至中式英語混用，缺乏一個統一的標準。教育國際化已經成爲必然趨勢，編者建議國內學校校名翻譯參考英美國家學校校名翻譯的方式。

1. 學前教育

英國學前托幼機構名稱及種類繁多，有招收 2~5 歲孩子的"Nursery"（幼兒園/托兒所），如托幼一體的：Ongar Nursery（央格爾幼兒園），也有招收 4~5 歲孩子的稱作"Infant School"的幼兒園，如：Fulwell Infant School（富爾韋爾幼兒園）等。美國幼兒園一般稱爲"Kindergarten"，招收 4~5 歲的孩子，如紐約地區著名的 Dalton Kindergarten（達爾頓幼兒園）。國內幼兒園名稱翻譯可以以此作爲參考，如：彩虹幼兒園，可以直接用漢語拼音音譯，翻譯爲 Caihong Nursery 或者 Caihong Kindergarten。

2. 初等教育

英國一般把小學稱作"Primary"或"Primary School"，多招收 4/5~11 歲的學生，如倫敦地區著名的小學 Bousfield Primary School（鮑斯菲爾德小學）。在美國，一般稱小學爲"Elementary"，如洛杉磯地區的 Pacific Elementary（太平洋小學），Turtle Rock Elementary（龜石小學）。也有一些學校冠全名"Elementary School"，如：Pantera Elementary School（範特拉小學）。國內小學名稱翻譯可參照此進行，如：彩虹小學，可以直接用拼音翻譯爲 Caihong Primary（School）或者 Caihong Elementary（School），若喜歡彩虹的含義，也可將對應的英文譯出，翻譯爲 Rainbow Primary（School）或者 Rainbow Elementary（School）。

3. 中等教育

　　英美國家中學規模一般不大，主要按年級區分，大多將初高中統整於一體，冠名"School"，分男校、女校和混合三種不同的類型。從校名上很難分辨某個中學是初中還是高中，如位於美國馬薩諸塞州的 The Cambridge School of Weston（威斯頓劍橋中學）是一所知名高中。有的學校也會在校名中標明性質，如英國著名的 St. Paul's Girls' School（聖保羅女子中學）。美國的 Secondary School（中學）一般由兩個階段課程組成：第一階段 middle school 或 junior high school，類似中國的"初中"，第二階段 high school，類似中國的"高中"。美國普遍的高中冠名是"High School"，如位於密歇根州的知名高中合校 Holland Christian High School（赫蘭克裡斯汀中學），位於內華達州的知名高中合校 Henderson International High School（亨德森國際學校）等。英美國家還有冠名爲"Academy"的中學，主要是學術性高中。甚至有冠名爲"College"的中學，如英國最著名的貴族學校 Eton College（伊頓公學）。

　　翻譯國內中學名稱時可參照英美中學最常規做法，尤其是相對簡潔的美國做法。比如：成都實驗外國語學校包含初高中，可將之統一翻譯爲：Chengdu Experimental Foreign Languages School；成都石室中學是一所著名高中，可翻譯爲：Chengdu Shishi High School；珠海市紫荊中學是一所初中，可譯爲 Zhuhai Zijing Middle School；珠海市一中是一所高中，可翻譯爲 Zhuhai No.1 High School。一些高校有附屬中學，如著名的北京師範大學附屬中學，可譯爲 The High School Affiliated to Beijing Normal University。

4. 高等教育

英美高等教育有着世界聞名的學術聲譽與地位。英國著名大學有劍橋大學（University of Cambridge）、牛津大學（University of Oxford）、杜倫大學（Durham University）、伯明翰大學（University of Birmingham）、倫敦政治經濟學院（London School of Economics and Political Science）等。美國著名大學有普林斯頓大學（Princeton University）、哈佛大學（Harvard University）、芝加哥大學（University of Chicago）、麻省理工學院（Massachusetts Institute of Technology）、加州理工學院（California Institute of Technology）、加州大學伯克利分校（University of California-Berkeley）、密歇根大學安娜堡分校（University of Michigan-Ann Arbor）等。

翻譯國內高校名稱時，格式上可參考英美大學名稱格式進行。比如：北京大學、清華大學可參照普林斯頓大學（Princeton University）、哈佛大學（Harvard University）格式，分別將之翻譯爲 Beijing University 與 Tsinghua University；北京航空航天大學可參照倫敦政治經濟學院（London School of Economics and Political Science）的格式翻譯爲 Beijing University of Aeronautics and Astronautics，中國政法大學可翻譯爲 China University of Political Science and Law；成都理工大學可參照加州理工學院（California Institute of Technology）的格式翻譯爲 Chengdu University of Technology。

需要指出的是，高校名稱翻譯不是一件簡單的事情，雖然翻譯格式可以參考國外高校，但是選詞用詞需仔細斟酌。比如：漢語的"大學/學院"在英語中有好些詞可表示，常見的有 university、college、institute、academy 等。翻譯校名之前，應先搞清楚幾個詞的含義和區別，還應對所要翻譯的學校有一定的瞭解，如學校的性質、規模、學術方向等，這樣才能做到翻譯準確。

二、各級各類學校名稱翻譯

托兒所/幼兒園　nursery / kindergarten
小學　primary school / elementary school
中學　middle school / secondary school
初中　junior middle school / junior high school
高中　senior middle school / senior high school
實驗中學　experimental middle school
職業中學　vocational middle school
大學/綜合性大學　university
學院（單科大學）　college
（專科）學院　academy
（理工科的）學院　institute
中等職業學校　secondary vocational school
中等技術學校　secondary technical school
高等職業技術學院　higher vocational and technical college
特殊教育學校　charter school / special education school
聾啞學校　school for the deaf-mutes
盲人學校　school for the blind
幼兒師範學校　school for kindergarten teachers
重點中學　key middle school
業餘學校　spare-time school

附屬學校　affiliated school
技工學校　vestibule school
護士學校　nursing school
公立學校　public school
私立學校　private school
示範中學　model middle school
文科大學　university of liberal arts
理科大學　university of science
綜合性大學　comprehensive university
函授學校　correspondence school
補習學校　continuation school
成人學校　adult school
老年大學　university for the aged
民辦學校　non-governmental school / school run by the local people
夜校　evening (night) school
假日學校　day school
寄宿學校　boarding school
財經學院　institute of finance and economics
師範學院　normal college
農學院　agricultural college
農業大學　agricultural university
文學院　college of arts
理學院　college of science
文理學院　college of arts and science
理工科大學　university of science and engineering
電子工程學院　institute of electronic engineering

電子工程大學　university of electronic engineering
電力工程學院　institute of electrical engineering
電訊工程學院　institute of telecommunications engineering
輕工業學院　institute of light industry
城建學院　institute of urban construction
測繪學院　institute of surveying and mapping
鐵道學院　railway institute
航空學院　aeronautical engineering institute
航空大學　aeronautical engineering university
郵電學院　institute of post and telecommunications
郵電大學　university of post and telecommunications
化工學院　institute of chemical engineering
化工大學　university of chemical engineering
法學院　college of law
政法大學　university of political science and law
醫學院　college of medicine
醫科大學　medical university / university of medicine
海洋學院　oceanography college
海洋大學　oceanography university
水產技術學校　marine products technical school
漁業航海學校　fishery and navigation school
水產大學　university of aquatic products
水利學院　institute of water-conservancy
氣象學院　meteorological institute
機械學院　college of mechanical engineering
機械工程大學　university of mechanical engineering

石油學院	petroleum college
石油大學	petroleum university
礦業學院	college of mining technology
礦業大學	university of mining technology
工業學院	polytechnic institute
工業大學	polytechnic university
林業學院	forestry institute
林業大學	forestry university
體育學院	institute of physical culture
體育大學	university of physical culture
商學院	college of commerce
工商大學	university of industry and commerce (business)
民族學院	institute for nationalities
民族大學	university for nationalities
廣播學院	institute of radio broadcasting
廣播電視大學	university of radio and television
外語學院	foreign languages college
外國語大學	foreign languages university
警官學院	college for police officers
警官大學	university for police officers
軍醫大學	university of army medicine
中醫學院	institute of Chinese traditional medicine
中醫藥大學	university of Chinese traditional medicine
教育學院	educational college
藝術學院	academy of arts
美術學院	academy of fine arts

戲曲學院　opera college

舞蹈學院　dancing college

音樂學院　conservatory of music

紡織工學院　institute of textile engineering

糧食工學院　institute of grain industry

船舶工學院　institute of ship-building engineering

建築工程學院　college of civil engineering

動力與能源學院　college of power and energy engineering

自動化學院　college of automation

水聲工程學院　college of underwater acoustic engineering

計算機科學與技術學院　college of computer and technology

機電工程學院　college of mechanical and electrical engineering

信息與通信工程學院　college of information and communications engineering

經濟管理學院　school of economics and management

材料科學與化學工程學院　college of material science and chemical engineering

核科學與技術學院　college of nuclear science and technology

人文社會科學學院　college of humanities and social sciences

冶金學院　metallurgy institute

絲綢工學院　institute of silk textile engineering

民用航空學院　institute for civil aviation

國際關係學院　college of international relations

教師進修學院　teacher's college for vocational studies

三、中國主要高校名稱翻譯

清華大學　Tsinghua University
北京大學　Peking University
中國人民大學　Renmin University of China
中央財經大學　The Central University of Finance and Economics
對外經濟貿易大學　University of International Business and Economics
北京外國語大學　Beijing Foreign Studies University
北京航空航天大學　Beijing University of Aeronautics and astronautics
北京師範大學　Beijing Normal University
中國政法大學　China University of Political Science and Law
北京郵電大學　Beijing University of Posts and Telecommunications
北京理工大學　Beijing Institute of Technology
北京交通大學　Beijing Jiaotong University
北京工業大學　Beijing University of Technology
北京科技大學　University of Science and Technology Beijing
北京化工大學　Beijing University of Chemical Technology
北京林業大學　Beijing Forestry University
中國傳媒大學　Communication University of China
中央音樂學院　Central Conservatory of Music
中央民族大學　Minzu University of China
北京體育大學　Beijing Sport University
中國農業大學　China Agricultural University

北京中醫藥大學　Beijing University of Chinese Medicine
北京語言大學　Beijing Language and Culture University
中國協和醫科大學　Chinese Peking Union Medical College
中國地質大學　China University of Geosciences
華北電力大學　North China Electric Power University
南開大學　Nankai University
天津大學　Tianjin University
天津醫科大學　Tianjin Medical University
天津外國語大學　Tianjin Foreign Studies University
天津商業大學　Tianjin University of Commerce
天津工業大學　Tianjin University of Technology
天津科技大學　Tianjin University of Science and Technology
天津城建大學　Tianjin Chengjian University
天津中醫藥大學　Tianjin University of Traditional Chinese Medicine
天津師範大學　Tianjin Normal University
天津財經大學　Tianjin University of Finance and Economics
河北工業大學　Hebei University of Technology
河北科技大學　Hebei University of Science and Technology
承德醫學院　Chengde Medical College
河北經貿大學　Hebei University of Business and Economics
河北金融學院　Hebei Finance University
河北建築工程學院　Hebei University of Architecture
河北大學　Hebei University
河北師範大學　Hebei Normal University
河北醫科大學　Hebei Medical University
河北農業大學　Hebei Agricultural University

燕山大學　Yanshan University

中國人民武裝警察部隊學院　Chinese People's Armed Police Force Academy

中央司法警官學院　Central Judicial Police Academy

太原理工大學　Taiyuan University of Technology

山西醫科大學　Shanxi Medical University

山西財經大學　Shanxi University of Finance and Economics

山西中醫學院　Shanxi University of Traditional Chinese medicine

太原科技大學　Taiyuan University of Science and Technology

山西大學　Shanxi University

山西師範大學　Shanxi Normal University

山西農業大學　Shanxi Agricultural University

內蒙古大學　Inner Mongolia University

內蒙古醫科大學　Inner Mongolia Medical University

內蒙古工業大學　Inner Mongolia University of Technology

內蒙古科技大學　Inner Mongolia University Of Science and Technology

內蒙古農業大學　Inner Mongolia Agricultural University

內蒙古師範大學　Inner Mongolia Normal University

內蒙古財經大學　Inner Mongolia University of Finance and Economics

內蒙古民族大學　Inner Mongolia University for Nationalities

大連理工大學　Dalian University of Technology

東北大學　Northeastern University

大連海事大學　Dalian Maritime University

遼寧大學　Liaoning University

沈陽醫學院　Shenyang Medical College

大連外國語大學　Dalian University of Foreign Languages
大連海洋大學　Dalian Ocean University
大連醫科大學　Dalian Medical University
東北財經大學　Dongbei University of Finance and Economics
大連大學　Dalian University
瀋陽大學　Shenyang University
遼寧工程技術大學　Liaoning Technical University
吉林大學　Jilin University
延邊大學　Yanbian University
東北師範大學　Northeast Normal University
吉林財經大學　Jilin University of Finance and Economics
東北電力大學　Northeast Electric Power University
吉林建築大學　Jilin Jianzhu University
長春中醫藥大學　Changchun University of Chinese Medicine
吉林農業大學　Jilin Agricultural University
哈爾濱工業大學　Harbin University of Technology
哈爾濱工程大學　Harbin Engineering University
東北林業大學　Northeast Forestry University
東北農業大學　Northeast Agricultural University
哈爾濱商業大學　Harbin University of Commerce
哈爾濱醫科大學　Harbin Medical University
哈爾濱理工大學　Harbin University of Science and Technology
黑龍江大學　Heilongjiang University
復旦大學　Fudan University
上海交通大學　Shanghai Jiao Tong University
同濟大學　Tongji University

上海財經大學　Shanghai University of Finance and Economics

上海外國語大學　Shanghai International Studies University

華東理工大學　East China University of Science

東華大學　Donghua University

上海大學　Shanghai University

華東師範大學　East China Normal University

中國人民解放軍第二軍醫大學　The Second Military Medical University

上海師範大學　Shanghai Normal University

上海理工大學　Shanghai University of Technology

上海工程技術大學　Shanghai University of Engineering Science

上海海事大學　Shanghai Maritime University

上海對外貿易學院　Shanghai Institute of Foreign Trade

華東政法學院　East China University of Politics and Law

上海體育學院　Shanghai University of Sport

上海音樂學院　Shanghai Conservatory of Music

上海戲劇學院　Shanghai Theatre Academy

南京大學　Nanjing University

東南大學　Southeast University

南京航空航天大學　Nanjing University of Aeronautics and Astronautics

蘇州大學　Suzhou University

河海大學　Hohai University

南京理工大學　Nanjing University of Science and Technology

中國藥科大學　China Pharmaceutical University

中國礦業大學　China University of Mining and Technology

江南大學　Jiangnan University

南京師範大學　Nanjing Normal University

南京農業大學　Nanjing Agricultural University

浙江大學　Zhejiang University

溫州大學　Wenzhou University

浙江理工大學　Zhejiang University of Technology

浙江工業大學　Zhejiang University of Technology

浙江師範大學　Zhejiang Normal University

杭州大學　Hangzhou University

杭州電子科技大學　Hangzhou University of Electronic Science and Technology

寧波大學　Ningbo University

中國科學技術大學　University of Science and Technology of China

安徽大學　Anhui University

合肥工業大學　Hefei University of Technology

安徽醫科大學　Anhui Medical University

安徽財經大學　Anhui University of Finance and Economics

安徽工業大學　Anhui University of Technology

安徽建築大學　Anhui Jianzhu University

安徽師範大學　Anhui Normal University

安徽農業大學　Anhui Agricultural University

廈門大學　Xiamen University

福州大學　Fuzhou University

福建警察學院　Fujian Police College

集美大學　Jimei University

福建醫科大學　Fujian Medical University

福建師範大學　Fujian Normal University

福建中醫藥大學　Fujian University of Traditional Chinese Medicine

福建農林大學　Fujian Agriculture and Forestry University

南昌大學　Nanchang University

南昌航空大學　Nanchang Hangkong University

江西中醫藥大學　Jiangxi University of Traditional Chinese Medicine

江西師範大學　Jiangxi Normal University

東華理工大學　East China University of Technology

江西財經大學　Jiangxi University of Finance and Economics

江西農業大學　Jiangxi Agricultural University

江西理工大學　Jiangxi University of Science and Technology

山東大學　Shandong University

中國海洋大學　Ocean University of China

中國石油大學　China University of Petroleum

山東財經大學　Shandong University of Finance and Economics

濟南大學　Jinan University

青島大學　Qingdao University

山東科技大學　Shandong University of Science and Technology

山東農業大學　Shandong Agricultural University

山東中醫藥大學　Shandong Traditional Chinese Medicine University

山東師範大學　Shandong Normal University

鄭州大學　Zhengzhou University

河南大學　Henan University

河南理工大學　Henan University of Technology

河南科技大學　Henan University of Science and Technology

河南工業大學　Henan University of Technology

河南師範大學　Henan Normal University
河南農業大學　Henan Agricultural University
武漢大學　Wuhan University
華中科技大學　Huazhong University of Science and Technology
中南財經政法大學　Zhongnan University of Economics & Law
湖北大學　Hubei University
華中農業大學　Huazhong Agricultural University
華中師範大學　Central China Normal University
武漢理工大學　Wuhan University of Technology
武漢科技大學　Wuhan University Of Science and Technology
中南民族大學　South-Central University for Nationalities
湖南大學　Hunan University
中南大學　Central South University
湖南師範大學　Hunan Normal University
湖南科技大學　Hunan University of Science and Technology
湖南農業大學　Hunan Agricultural University
長沙理工大學　Changsha University of Technology
中國科學技術大學　University of Science and Technology of China
國防科學技術大學　National University of Defense Technology
中國海洋大學　Chinese Marine University
廣州大學　Guangzhou University
中山大學　Sun Yat-Sen University / Zhongshan University
暨南大學　Jinan University
深圳大學　Shenzhen University
汕頭大學　Shantou University
廣東工業大學　Guangdong University of Technology

廣州中醫藥大學　Guangzhou University of Traditional Chinese Medicine

華南理工大學　South China University of Technology

華南師範大學　South China Normal University

華南農業大學　South China Agricultural University

廣西大學　Guangxi University

廣西醫科大學　Guangxi Medical University

廣西師範大學　Guangxi Normal University

海南大學　Hainan University

海南師範大學　Hainan Normal University

海南醫學院　Hainan Medical College

華南熱帶農業大學　South China University of Tropical Agriculture

重慶大學　Chongqing University

西南大學　Southwestern University

重慶醫科大學　Medical University of Chongqing

重慶工商大學　Industrial and Commercial University of Chongqing

重慶師範大學　Chongqing Normal University

重慶交通大學　Chongqing Jiaotong University

重慶郵電大學　Chongqing University of Post and Telecommunications

西南政法大學　Southwest University of Political Science and Law

四川外國語大學　Sichuan International Studies University

四川大學　Sichuan University

西南財經大學　Southwestern University of Finance and Economics

西南交通大學　Southwest Jiaotong University

電子科技大學　University of Electronic Science and Technology of China

四川農業大學　Sichuan Agricultural University
成都中醫藥大學　Chengdu University of Traditional Chinese Medicine
成都理工大學　Chengdu University of Technology
西南石油大學　Southwest Petroleum University
成都信息工程大學　Chengdu University of Information Technology
四川師範大學　Sichuan Normal University
西南民族大學　Southwest University for Nationalities
成都體育學院　Chengdu University of Sport
四川音樂學院　Sichuan Academy of Music
中國民用航空學院　Civil Aeronautical Engineering Institutes of China
西南科技大學　Southwest University of Science and Technology
貴州大學　Guizhou University
貴州財經大學　Guizhou University of Finance and Economics
貴州師範大學　Guizhou Normal University
貴州醫科大學　Guizhou Medical University
雲南大學　Yunnan University
雲南財經大學　Yunnan University of Finance and Economics
昆明理工大學　Kunming University of Science and Technology
昆明醫科大學　Kunming Medical University
雲南師範大學　Yunnan Normal University
雲南警官學院　Yunnan Police Officer Academy
西南林業大學　Yunnan Forestry University
雲南民族大學　Yunnan University for Nationalities
西藏大學　Tibet University
西安交通大學　Xi'an Jiaotong University

西北工業大學　Northwestern Polytechnical University

西安電子科技大學　Xidian University

長安大學　Chang'an University

西北大學　Northeast University

西北農林科技大學　Northwest Agriculture and Forestry University

陝西師範大學　Shaanxi Normal University

中國人民解放軍第四軍醫大學　The Fourth Military Medical University

蘭州大學　Lanzhou University

寧夏大學　Ningxia University

蘭州交通大學　Lanzhou Jiaotong University

蘭州理工大學　Lanzhou University of Technology

西北師範大學　Northwest Normal University

蘭州財經大學　Lanzhou University of Finance and Economics

甘肅農業大學　Gansu Agricultural University

西北民族大學　Northwest University for Nationalities

新疆大學　Xinjiang University

香港中文大學　The Chinese University of Hong Kong

香港科技大學　The Hong Kong University of Science and Technology

澳門大學　University of Macau / Universidade de Macau

四、學位名稱翻譯

學士學位　bachelor's degree

碩士學位	master's degree
博士學位	doctoral degree
法學博士	doctor of law
文學博士	doctor of arts
哲學博士	doctor of philosophy
理學博士	doctor of science
醫學博士	doctor of medicine
博士後	postdoctoral student
文學碩士	master of arts
理學碩士	master of science
醫學碩士	master of medicine
工程碩士	master of engineering
建築碩士	master of architecture
農學碩士	master of agriculture
法學碩士	master of law
美術碩士	master of fine arts
哲學碩士	master of philosophy
藥學碩士	master of pharmacy
新聞碩士	master of journalism
會計學碩士	master of accounting
工商管理碩士	master of business administration
圖書館學碩士	master of library science
公共衛生碩士	master of public health
工學學士	bachelor of engineering
文學學士	bachelor of arts（BA）
理學學士	bachelor of science（BS）

法學學士　bachelor of law（BL）
醫學學士　bachelor of medicine（BM）
藥學學士　bachelor of pharmacy（BP）
農學學士　bachelor of agriculture（BA）
美術學士　bachelor of fine arts（BFA）
音樂學士　bachelor of music（BM）
工商學士　bachelor of business administration

五、學科及專業名稱翻譯

哲學 Philosophy

哲學　Philosophy
中國哲學　Chinese Philosophy
外國哲學　Foreign Philosophy
馬克思主義哲學　Philosophy of Marxism
邏輯學　Logic
倫理學　Ethics
美學　Aesthetics
宗教學　Science of Religion
科學技術哲學　Philosophy of Science and Technology

經濟學 Economics

經濟學　Economics

政治經濟學　Political Economics
理論經濟學　Theoretical Economics
馬克思主義經濟學　Marxist Economics
經濟史　History of Economy
世界經濟學　World Economics
西方經濟學　Western Economics
應用經濟學　Applied Economics
國民經濟學　National Economics
區域經濟學　Regional Economics
財政學（含稅收學）　Public Finance / Fiscal Science（including Taxation）
金融學（含保險學）　Finance（including Insurance）
產業經濟學　Industrial Economics
國際貿易學　International Trade
勞動經濟學　Labor Economics
統計學　Statistics
國防經濟學　National Defense Economics

法學 Law / Science of Law / Legal Science

法學　Law
法律史　Legal History / History of Law
憲法學與行政法學　Constitutional Law and Administrative Law
刑法學　Science of Criminal Law / Criminal Jurisprudence
訴訟法學　Science of Procedure Laws / Litigation Law
經濟法學　Science of Economic Law / Law of Economy

民商法學　Civil Law and Commercial Law
環境與資源保護法學　Science of Environment and Natural Resources Protection Law
國際法學　International law
軍事法學　Science of Military Law

政治學 Political Science

政治學　Political Science
政治學理論　Political Theory
中共黨史　History of the Communist Party of China
馬克思主義理論與思想政治教育　Education of Marxist Theory and Education in Ideology and Politics
國際政治學　International Politics
國際關係學　International Relations

社會學 Sociology

社會學　Sociology
人口學　Demography
人類學　Anthropology
民俗學（含中國民間文學）　Folklore（including Chinese Folk Literature）

民族學 Ethnology

民族學　Ethnology

馬克思主義民族理論與政策　Marxist Ethnic Theory and Policy
中國少數民族史　Chinese Ethnic History
中國少數民族經濟　Chinese Ethnic Economics
中國少數民族藝術　Chinese Ethnic Art

教育學 Education / Education Science

教育學　Education Science / Pedagogy
教育學原理　Educational Principle
課程與教學論　Curriculum and Teaching Methodology
教育史　History of Education
高等教育學　Higher Education / Higher Pedagogy / Tertiary Education
成人教育學　Adult Education / Andragogy
職業技術教育學　Vocational and Technical Education
特殊教育學　Special Education
教育技術學　Educational Technology
心理學　Psychology
基礎心理學　Basic Psychology
應用心理學　Applied Psychology
體育學　Physical Education / Science of Physical Culture and Sports
體育人文社會學　Humanistic and Sociological Science of Sports
運動人體科學　Human Movement Science / Human Kinetic Science
體育教育訓練學　Theory of Sports Pedagogy and Training
民族傳統體育學　Science of Ethnic Traditional Sports

文學 Literature

文學　Literature
中國語言文學　Chinese Literature
文藝學　Theory of Literature and Art
語言學及應用語言學　Linguistics and Applied Linguistics
漢語言文字學　Chinese Philology
中國古典文獻學　Ancient Chinese Philology
中國古代文學　Ancient Chinese Literature
中國現當代文學　Chinese Modern and Contemporary Literature
中國少數民族語言文學　Chinese Ethnic Language and Literature
比較文學與世界文學　Comparative Literature and World Literature
外國語言文學　Foreign Languages and Literatures
英語語言文學　English Language and Literature
俄語語言文學　Russian Language and Literature
法語語言文學　French Language and Literature
德語語言文學　German Language and Literature
日語語言文學　Japanese Language and Literature
印度語言文學　Indian Language and Literature
西班牙語語言文學　Spanish Language and Literature
阿拉伯語語言文學　Arabic Language and Literature
歐洲語言文學　European Language and Literature
亞非語言文學　Asian-African Language and Literature
外國語言學及應用語言學　Foreign Linguistics and Applied Linguistics

藝術學 Art

藝術學　Art Theory
音樂學　Music / Musicology
美術學　Fine Arts
設計藝術學　Artistic Design
戲劇戲曲學　Theater and Chinese Traditional Opera
電影學　Film / Filmology
廣播電視藝術學　Radio and Television Art
舞蹈學　Dance / Dancology

歷史學 History

歷史學　History
史學理論及史學史　Historical Theories and History of Historiography
考古學及博物館學　Archaeology and Museology
歷史地理學　Historical Geography
歷史文獻學　Studies of Historical Literature / Historical Philology
專門史　Specialized History / History of Particular Subjects
通史　General History
中國史通論　General Theory of Chinese History
世界史通論　General Theory of the World History
中國古代史　Ancient Chinese History
中國近現代史　Modern and Contemporary Chinese History
世界史　World History

理學 Natural Science

理學　Natural Science

數學　Mathematics

基礎數學　Fundamental Mathematics / Pure Mathematics

計算數學　Computational Mathematics / Calculus Mathematics

概率論與數理統計　Probability and Mathematical Statistics

應用數學　Applied Mathematics

物理學　Physics

理論物理　Theoretical Physics

粒子物理與原子核物理　Particle Physics and Nuclear Physics

原子與分子物理　Atomic and Molecular Physics

聲學　Acoustics

光學　Optics

化學　Chemistry

有機化學　Organic Chemistry

無機化學　Inorganic Chemistry

分析化學　Analytical Chemistry

物理化學（含化學物理）　Physical Chemistry（including Chemical Physics）

高分子化學與物理　Polymeric Chemistry and Physics

天文學　Astronomy

天體物理　Astrophysics

天體測量與天體力學　Astrometry and Celestial Mechanics

地理學　Geography

自然地理學　Physical Geography / Physiography
人文地理學　Human Geography
氣象學　Meteorology
海洋學　Oceanography / Marine Science
地質學　Geology
礦物學　Mineralogy
岩石學　Petrology
構造地質學　Structural Geology
生物學　Biology
植物學　Botany
動物學　Zoology
生理學　Physiology
微生物學　Microbiology
神經生物學　Neurobiology
遺傳學　Genetics
細胞生物學　Cell Biology
生物化學與分子生物學　Biochemistry and Molecular Biology
生物物理學　Biophysics
生態學　Ecology

工學 Engineering

工學　Engineering
力學　Mechanics
工程力學　Engineering Mechanics
車輛工程　Vehicle Engineering

光學工程　Optical Engineering
材料科學與工程　Materials Science and Engineering
計算機科學與技術　Computer Science and Technology
計算機軟件與理論　Computer Software and Theory
計算機應用技術　Computer Applied Technology
電子信息科學與技術　Electronic Information Science and Technology
電子信息工程　Electronic Information Engineering
數字媒體技術　Digital Media Technology
通信工程　Communication Engineering
網路工程　Network Engineering
土木工程　Civil Engineering
市政工程　Municipal Engineering
橋樑與隧道工程　Bridge and Tunnel Engineering
水利工程　Hydraulic Engineering
測繪科學與技術　Surveying and Mapping
化學工程　Chemical Engineering
生物化工　Biochemical Engineering
地質工程　Geological Engineering
礦產普查與勘探　Mineral Resources Prospecting and Exploration
採礦工程　Mining Engineering
紡織工程　Textile Engineering
服裝設計與工程　Clothing Design and Engineering
輕工技術與工程　The Light Industry Technology and Engineering
交通運輸工程　Communication and Transportation Engineering
道路與鐵道工程　Highway and Railway Engineering
交通信息工程及控制　Traffic Information Engineering and Control

交通運輸規劃與管理　Transportation Planning and Management

核科學與技術　Nuclear Science and Technology

農業工程　Agricultural Engineering

農業機械化工程　Agricultural Mechanization Engineering

林業工程　Forestry Engineering

環境科學與工程　Environmental Science and Engineering

生物醫學工程　Biomedical Engineering

食品科學與工程　Food Science and Engineering

農學 Agriculture

農學　Agriculture

作物學　Crop Science

作物栽培與耕作學　Crop Cultivation and Geoponics

作物遺傳育種學　Crop Genetics and Breeding

園藝學　Horticulture

農業資源利用學　Utilization Science of Agricultural Resources

土壤學　Soil Science

農藥學　Pesticide Science / Agricultural Pharmacology

畜牧學　Animal Science

獸醫學　Veterinary Medicine

林學　Forestry

水土保持與荒漠化防治　Soil and Water Conservation and Desertification Combating

管理學　Management

　　管理學　Management
　　管理科學與工程　Management Science and Engineering
　　工商管理學　Science of Business Administration
　　會計學　Accounting
　　企業管理學　Corporate Management
　　旅遊管理學　Tourism Management
　　公共管理學　Science of Public Management
　　行政管理學　Administration Management
　　社會醫學與衛生事業管理學　Social Medicine and Health Care Management
　　教育經濟與管理學　Educational Economy and Management
　　土地資源管理學　Land Resources Management
　　圖書館、情報與檔案學　Science of Library, Information and Archival

醫學 Medicine

　　醫學　Medicine
　　免疫學　Immunology
　　病理學　Pathology
　　法醫學　Forensic Medicine
　　放射醫學　Radiology / Radiation Medicine
　　臨床醫學　Clinical Medicine
　　內科學　Internal medicine

外科學　Surgery
兒科學　Pediatrics
老年醫學　Geriatrics
神經病學　Neurology
護理學　Nursing
婦產科學　Obstetrics and Gynecology
眼科學　Ophthalmology
耳鼻咽喉科學　Otolaryngology
腫瘤學　Oncology
理療學　Physical Therapy
康復醫學　Rehabilitation Medicine
運動醫學　Sports Medicine
麻醉學　Anesthesiology
急診醫學　Emergency Medicine
口腔醫學　Stomatology
公共衛生與預防醫學　Public Health and Preventive Medicine
流行病與衛生統計學　Epidemiology and Health Statistics
勞動衛生與環境衛生學　Occupational and Environmental Health
營養與食品衛生學　Nutrition and Food Hygiene
軍事預防醫學　Military Preventive Medicine
中醫學　Chinese Medicine
針灸學　Science of Acupuncture and Massage
藥學　Pharmacology
藥物化學　Medicinal Chemistry
藥劑學　Pharmacy / Pharmaceutics
藥理學　Pharmacology

中藥學　Chinese Pharmacology

軍事學　Military Science

軍事學　Military Science
軍事思想學　Military Ideology
軍事歷史學　Military History
戰略學　Science of Strategy
軍事戰略學　Military Strategy
戰役學　Science of Operations
聯合戰役學　Joint Operation
戰術學　Science of Tactics
合同戰術學　Combined-Arms Tactics
兵種戰術學　Branch Tactics
軍隊指揮學　Science of Military Command
軍事運籌學　Military Operation Research
軍事通信學　Military Communication
軍事情報學　Military Informatics
密碼學　Cryptography
軍事教育訓練（含軍事體育學）　Military Education and Training (including Military Physical Training)
軍制學　Science of Military System
軍事組織編制學　Military Organizational System
軍隊管理學　Military Management
軍隊政治工作學　Science of Military Political Work

六、教育常用術語翻譯

全民教育　education for the whole people
全日制教育　full-time education
義務教育　compulsory education
九年制義務教育　nine-year compulsory education
普及教育　universal education
學前教育　preschool education
職業教育　vocational education
應試教育　examination-oriented education
成人教育　adult education
政治教育　ideological education
國民教育　national education
幼兒園教育　kindergarten education
啟蒙教育　primary education
小學教育　primary school education
中等教育　secondary school education
高等教育　higher education / tertiary education
職業教育體系　vocational education system
遠程教育　distance education
函授教育　correspondence education
正規教育　formal education
網路教育　online education
品德教育　moral education

特殊教育　special education
普及義務教育　universal compulsory education
中等職業教育　secondary vocational education
德育及國民教育　moral and national education
高等教育"211工程"　the "211" project for higher education
高等教育"985工程"　the "985" project for higher education
因材施教原則　individualized instruction principle
學校管理體系　administration system for schools
教學質量評估　Teaching quality assessment
教師資格認定　accreditation of teacher's qualification
研究生課程班　non-degree postgraduate course
教育亂收費　unauthorized collections of fees by educational institutions
教育綜合改革　comprehensive education reform
考試招生制度　examination and enrollment systems
高校辦學自主權　Institutions of higher learning enjoy more decision-making power
教育扶貧工程　the project to alleviate poverty through education
農村義務教育　compulsory education in rural areas
品學兼優　excellent in character and learning
教學原則　teaching principles
教學計劃　teaching plan
教學管理　teaching administration
教學大綱　teaching syllabus
評教評學　assessment on teaching and learning
課程體系　curriculum system
升學考試　promotion examination

畢業考試　graduation examination
期中考試　mid-term examination
期終考試　final examination
全國統考　national unified examination
全國統一高考　national unified college and university entrance examination
文科綜合考試　integrated examination for social science
理科綜合考試　integrated examination for science
考大學　to take a college entrance examination
考上大學　to be admitted to a university
社會力量辦學　to manage schools by social resources
定向招生　recruitment of students from selected departments or regions
定向培養　to provide training to selected students
同等學歷　academic qualification equivalent
畢業實習　graduation field work
畢業論文　graduation dissertation
畢業設計　graduation project
畢業證書　graduation certificate
畢業典禮　graduation ceremony / commencement
畢業分配　job assignment on graduation
必修課　compulsory course
選修課　optional course
基礎課　basic course
專業課　specialized course
課程表　schedule / school timetable

主修英語　to major in English

考勤　to check on class attendance

考題　examination questions

考卷　examination paper

考取　to pass an entrance examination

考生　examinee / a candidate for an entrance examination

學制　school system

休學　schooling suspension

逃學/曠課　to skip classes / to play truant

轉學　to transfer to another school

退學　to leave school / to discontinue one's schooling

勒令退學　to be ordered to quit school

學科　discipline / a school subject

學籍　one's status as a student

學費　tuition fee

學生證　student's identity card

學分　credit

學分制　credit system

學風　academic atmosphere

學會　learned society

學派　school of thought

學歷　academic credentials

學時　class hour

學期　school term / semester

學年　academic year

學位　academic degree

學者　scholar / a learned man
成績單　school report
通車生　day student / non-resident student
住宿生　boarder
旁聽生　auditor
校友　alumnus / alumna
小學生　primary school pupil
中學生　middle school student
大學生　university / college student
中專生　secondary specialized school student
大專生　professional training college student
大學本科生　university / college undergraduate
大學學歷　college / university degree
大一學生　freshman
大二學生　sophomore
大三學生　junior
大四學生　senior
研究生　postgraduate (student) / graduate student
《大學生守則》　Rules for College Students

第二單元
公共標識語

隨著中國與世界的接軌，越來越多的國人走出了國門。與此同時，來中國旅遊、經商、工作、學習的國際友人與日俱增，跨國、跨文化交流也日益增多。英語作爲國際通用語，滲透到社會生活的各個領域，其重要性日益增強，使用範圍日益擴大。安全標誌、交通標誌、公用設施標誌，特別是旅遊景區、車站、商場、學校等地的漢英雙語標識越來越多，公共標識語雙語化已漸成趨勢。英文標示語是城市國際化的一種標誌，也是國際友人瞭解中國的窗口，可以折射出一個城市的文化底蘊、市民的綜合素質、政府的管理能力以及社會的文明水平等。標識語翻譯的重要性不言而喻。

本單元簡單介紹公共標識語的特點和主要表現形式，公共標識語的幾種英譯方式以及幾類與讀者生活密切相關的標識語翻譯，如通用標識語、道路交通標識語、旅遊景區景點標識語、文教衛生標識語以及常見公益廣告。

一、公共標識語的特點及表現形式

公共標識具有簡明性、功能性、規約性、正式性、規範性等特點。簡潔明確是公共標識最大的特點。標識語一般用於公共場所，其功能是以簡單易懂和準確無誤的語言給受眾傳遞特定的信息。

英文公共標識一般有三種常用表現形式：獨立詞語（Independent Words）、短語（Phrases）以及完整句（Sentences）。獨立詞語即由單個英文詞語構成的獨立標誌，有比較鮮明的規約性，所用詞語具有約定俗成的特點。例如北美地區高速公路、街道兩旁設立的交通標識，多爲獨立詞語，如"Yield"（禮讓行駛）、"Shoulder"（路肩）。短語構成的英文公共標識一般有帶否定詞與不帶否定詞兩種形式。帶否定詞的短語，通常表示"禁止"，如"No Visitors"（謝絕來訪），"No Left Turn"（禁止左轉）。不帶否定詞的短語，通常表示"必須"，如"Emergency Exit Only"（緊急出口，險情專用），"Bus Parking Only"（公車停車專用）。短語形式構成的公共標識一般有"名詞短語"與"分詞短語"兩種。名詞短語如"Taxi Lane"（計程車道），"Pedestrian Crosswalk"（人行橫道）等，分詞短語如"Unauthorized Vehicles Prohibited"（外部車輛，禁止入內），"No Littering"（請勿亂扔垃圾）等。完整句式指由一個完整句子所構成的英文公共標識，具有較充分的説明性與指示性特點，一般也有肯定式與否定式兩種。肯定式如"All Visitors Must Register"（來客登記），"Turning Traffic Must Yield To Pedestrians"（轉彎車輛，禮讓行人），"Children Must Be Accompanied By An Adult"（兒童要有成人陪同）等。否定式如"In Case Of Fire, Do Not Use Elevators. Use Stairways"（如遇火警，勿乘電梯，請走樓梯逃生）等。

二、公共標識語常用的幾種英譯方式

1. "… + Only"
公車專用道　Buses Only
貴賓專用　Distinguished Guests Only
員工通道　Staff Only
僅作火警安全出口　Fire Exit Only
送客止步　Passengers Only
殘疾人專用車位　Disabled Parking Only
禁止車輛通行　Pedestrians Only

2. "No + -ing 分詞"
電梯內嚴禁吸烟　No Smoking In Elevators
請勿隨地吐痰　No Spitting
酒後勿駕駛　No Drunk Driving
不要超車　No Overtaking
請勿亂扔垃圾　No Littering
禁止跨越護欄　No Climbing Over The Fence

3. "No + 名詞"
禁止左/右轉　No Left / Right Turn
禁止掉頭　No U-Turn
請勿使用閃光燈　No Flash Photography
禁止寵物入內　No Pets
謝絕參觀/遊客止步　No Admittance
飲料食物，謝絕入內　No Food Or Drink

4. 使用名詞短語

單行道　One Way Street

計程車道　Taxi Lane

前方學校　School Ahead

人行橫道　Pedestrian Crosswalk

旅遊紀念品商店　Souvenir Shop

5. 使用祈使句

請勿扶圍欄　Take Your Hands Off The Rails

門廊勿放自行車　Keep This Doorway Free Of Bikes

請保管好自己的物品　Take Care Of Your Belongings

請在安全線內候車　Stay Behind The Yellow Line

變換車道, 注意後車　Look Back Before Changing Lanes

請勿亂扔垃圾　Please Do Not Litter

請勿觸摸　Please Do Not Touch

嚴禁向窗外拋扔物品　Do Not Throw Trash Out Of Window

請勿進入　Do Not Go Inside

看管好您的個人財物　Take Care Of Your Personal Belongings / Do Not Leave Your Belongings Unattented

6. "注意…" "小心…" 可用 Caution：+ 名詞；Mind/Watch + 名詞

小心地滑　Caution：Wet Floor

油漆未乾　Caution：Wet / Fresh Paint

當心燙傷　Caution！Very Hot Water

小心碰頭　Mind Your Head / Watch Your Head

當心臺階　Mind The Step / Watch Your Step

當心來往車輛　Watch For Moving Vehicles

7. 使用比較正式文體

非本園車輛禁止入內　Unauthorized Vehicles Are Prohibited In This Park

本公園禁止停車　Parking Of Vehicles Is Prohibited In This Park

嚴禁攜帶危險品上車　Hazardous Articles Prohibited On Board

8. 關於街名標識（Street Name Signs）翻譯

街道類常見標誌有："大道"（Avenue）、"街"（Street）、"路"（Road）、"巷"（Lane）、"胡同"（Hutong）、"弄"（Long）、"廣場"（Square）、"商業廣場"（Plaza）、"橋"（Bridge）等。業界專家建議，在漢語街道名稱的英譯方面，可採用"遵守法規、分類處理、括注變通、標準得體"的綜合性原則。"遵守法規"，即遵循國家有關法律法規，在街道名稱英譯上，不論專名通名，一律採用"拼音化"方式處理。如"武侯大街"翻譯爲"Wuhou Dajie"。"分類處理"，即在翻譯含有地理名稱的服務性設施時，採用專名部分拼音化，通名部分英譯的方式。如"成都火車站"譯爲"Chengdu Railway Station"，"雙流機場"譯爲"Shuangliu Airport"。"括註變通"，即在拼音化的街道名稱之後加一個括號，註明括號裡是相應街道名稱通名的英文説法。如"武侯大街"譯爲"Wuhou Dajie（Avenue）"。"標準得體"，主要針對街道名稱通名部分"括註變通"翻譯而言。這部分應當參照英語國家街名標誌的用語習慣及規範標準來處理，與國際慣例接軌。如街/大街譯爲 Street，道/大道譯爲 Avenue，公路譯爲 Highway，高速公路譯爲 Expressway 等。

三、常見公共標識語翻譯

1. 通用標識語

拉　　PULL／Pull

推　　PUSH／Push

入口　　ENTRANCE／Entrance

出口／安全出口／安全通道　　EXIT／Exit

緊急出口　　Emergency Exit

當心觸電　　Danger！High Voltage

當心臺階　　Mind The Step／Watch Your Step

當心腳下　　Watch Your Step

小心玻璃　　Caution！Glass

小心滑倒／小心地滑　　Caution！Slippery／Caution！Wet Floor

小心碰頭　　Mind Your Head／Watch Your Head

小心落物　　Danger！Falling Objects！

危險，請勿靠近　　Danger！Keep Away！

禁止停車　　No Parking

禁止停留　　No Stopping

禁止吸煙　　No Smoking

請勿跨越　　No Crossing

請勿拍照　　No Photography

請勿攝影　　No Filming／No Video

請勿使用閃光燈　　No Flash Photography

勿扔垃圾/請勿亂扔廢棄物　No Littering

請勿隨地吐痰　No Spitting

危險，請勿靠近　Danger! Keep Away

請勿打電話　No Phone Calls

請勿帶寵物入內　No Pets Allowed

請勿撫摸/請勿觸摸　Don't Touch

請勿踐踏草坪　Please Keep Off the Grass

請愛護公共財產　Please Protect Public Property

請愛護公共設施 Please Protect Public Facilities

請節約用水　Please Save Water / Don't Waste Water

請您保管好自己的物品　Take Care Of Your Belongings

請按順序排隊　Please Line Up

保持安靜/請勿大聲喧嘩　Quiet Please

廢物箱/垃圾箱　Trash / Litter

不可回收利用垃圾　Non-Recyclable

可回收利用垃圾　Recyclable

殘疾人專用　Disabled Only

留言欄　Complaints & Suggestions

伸手出水　Automatic Tap

公共廁所　Toilet / Washroom / Restroom

男廁所　Gents / Men

女廁所　Ladies / Women

有人（廁所）　Occupied

請便後衝洗　Flush After Use

乾手機　Hand Dryer

隨手關門　Keep Door Closed / Please Close The Door Behind You

節約用電（水）　Save On Electricity（Water）

禁止入內/嚴禁入內　No Entry / No Admittance

閑人免進/請勿入內　Staff Only / No Admittance

謝絕參觀/遊客止步　No Admittance

正在維修　Repairs In Progress

請繞行　Detour

有電危險　Danger! Electric Shock Risk

嚴禁攜帶易燃易爆等危險品　Dangerous Articles Prohibited

暫停服務/臨時關閉　Temporarily Closed

老年人、殘疾人優先　Priority For Seniors And Disabled

請在此等候　Please Wait Here

消防通道，請勿占用　Fire Engine Access. Don't Block！

停車場　Parking

醫務室　Clinic

步行梯/樓梯　Stairs

自動扶梯　Escalator

電梯　Elevator / Lift

問詢處/諮詢（臺）　Information

前臺/服務臺/接待　Reception

消防栓　Fire Hydrant

派出所　Police Station

緊急救護電話（120）　First Aid Call 120

緊急疏散地　Evacuation Site

急救中心　First Aid Center

公用電話　Telephone

磁卡電話　Magnetic Card Phone

投訴電話　Complaints Hotline

危難時請速報110　Emergency Call 110

員工通道　Staff Only

疏散通道　Escape Route

消防通道　Fire Engine Access

緊急呼救設施/緊急報警器　Emergency Alarm

自行車停放處　Bicycle Parking

計程車　Taxi

殘疾人設施　For Disabled

火情警報設施　Fire Alarm

緊急呼救電話　Emergency Phone

失物招領　Lost & Found

收銀臺/收款臺　Cashier

餐廳　Restaurant

商店　Shop

食品部　Food Shop

酒吧　Bar / Pub

快餐廳　Snack Bar / Fast Food

西餐廳　Western Restaurant

中餐廳　Chinese Restaurant

咖啡館/咖啡廳　Café

吸烟室　Smoking Room

一/二/三/四/五層（樓）　F1 / F2 / F3 / F4 / F5

地下一層/二層/三層　B1 / B2 / B3

滅火器　Fire Extinguisher

飲水處　Drinking Water

自動取款機　ATM

吸烟室　Smoking Room

營業時間　Business Hours

周末節假日不營業　Closed On Weekends And Public Holidays

試衣間　Fitting Room

留言板　Message（Bulletin）Board

服務中心　Service Center

行李寄存/存包處　Left Luggage / Luggage Storage

外幣兌換　Foreign Exchange

設備維修中　Under Maintenance

扶梯暫停使用　Escalator Out Of Service

洗手間清潔中，暫停使用　Restroom Closed For Cleaning

請打電話諮詢　Please Ring / Call / Phone For Assistance

火警電話　Fire Call 119 / Fire Alarm 119

安全疏散指示圖/緊急疏散指示圖　Evacuation Chart

如遇火警，勿乘電梯，請走樓梯逃生　In Case Of Fire, Do Not Use Elevators. Use Stairways

2. 道路交通標識語

登機信息查詢　Boarding Information

到達時間　Arrival Time

送客止步　Passengers Only

經濟艙　Economy Class

機場班車　Airport Shuttle

二樓候車室　Second Floor Waiting Room

國際中轉　International Connections

國內中轉　Domestic Connections

航班信息　Flight Information

出發航班　Departing Flights

行李提取處　Baggage Claim

行李安檢通道　Luggage Check

檢票處　Check-In

請讓工作人員驗票出站　Check-Out

嚴禁攜帶危險品上車　Hazardous Articles Prohibited On Board

嚴禁攜帶易燃易爆物品　No Inflammables Or Explosives

憑當日當次車票進站候車　Admission By Current Tickets

嚴禁向窗外拋扔物品　Do Not Throw Trash Out Of Window

請在安全線內候車　Stay Behind The Yellow Line

行李安檢通道　Luggage Check

抓牢扶手　Hold Handrail

老年人專座　Reserved For Seniors

老弱病殘專座　Courtesy Seats

老年人優先上車　Senior Citizens First

先下後上　Getting Off First

看管好您的個人財物　Take Care Of Your Personal Belongings / Do Not Leave Your Belongings Unattented

離開時帶好包　Take Your Bags When Leaving

斑馬線　Zebra Crossing / Pedestrian Crossing

步行街　Pedestrian Street

立交橋　Overpass

地道　Underground Passage / Underpass

地鐵　Subway

公車站　Bus Stop

機動車道：嚴禁自行車、摩托車和行人通行　Motor Vehicles Only

禁止自行車通行　No Bicycles

注意此路不通　Caution! No Thoroughfare

地下停車場收費處　Basement Parking Fare Collection

只準臨時停車下客　Drop-Off Only. No Parking

洗車　Car Wash

禁止鳴笛　No Horn

禁止車輛通行　Pedestrians Only

一慢，二看，三通過　Look Before Crossing

前方學校　School Ahead

嚴禁行人橫過馬路　No Jaywalking

追尾危險　Caution! Rear-End Collision

酒後勿駕駛　No Drunk Driving

嚴禁疲勞駕駛　No Fatigue Driving

請勿疲勞駕駛　Don't Drive When Tired

禁止超載　No Overloading

禁止掉頭　No U-Turn

保持車距　Keep Distance

道路擁擠，注意安全　Heavy Traffic. Drive Carefully

變換車道，註意後車　Look Back Before Changing Lanes

超車道　Fast Lane

嚴禁追尾　Do Not Follow Too Closely

車輛慢行　Slow Down

道路施工　Road Work Ahead

車輛繞行　Detour

雙向交通　Two-Way Traffic

單行交通　One-Way Traffic

禁止駛入/嚴禁通行　No Entry

禁止超越線　No Passing

此路不通　Dead End

計程車等候區域　Taxi Waiting Area

禁止左轉　No Left Turn

大型車靠右　Large Vehicles Keep Right

公共汽車優先　Bus Priority

請繫好安全帶　Buckle Up

換乘（機場、火車站）　Transit

換乘（計程車、公車）　Transfer

紅燈停，綠燈行　Stop On Red And Move On Green

乘客須知　Notice To Passengers

禁止在街道上玩耍　No Playing In The Street

禁止行人過街　No Pedestrians Crossing

前方校車停靠　School Bus Stop Ahead

殘疾人專用車位　Disabled Parking Only

產婦孕婦專用車位　Reserved Parking For New Mothers & Mothers To Be

車位已滿，請勿駛入　Parking Is Full. Do Not Enter

不要超車　Do Not Overtake / No Overtaking

道路擁擠，注意安全　Heavy Traffic. Drive Carefully

遵守法規，請系好安全帶　Buckle Up. It Is The Law

時速限制：每小時 30 千米　Speed Limit：30 km/h

减速缓行！人行道　Slow Down! Pedestrian Walkway

3. 旅遊景區景點標識語

景點開放　Open To Visitors

景點關閉　Closed To Visitors

珍惜文物古跡，勿亂刻亂涂　No Graffiti!

保護古跡，請勿觸摸　Protect Historic Site And Do Not Touch

保護文物，請勿刻畫　Protect Historic Site And Do Not Scratch

保護文物古跡，人人有責　Protection Of Historical Relics Is Everyone's Business

愛護綠化，請勿雕刻　Keep Off The Grass. No Carving On The Trees

禁止在牆上亂寫亂畫　No Scribbling On The Wall

請勿拍照　No Photography

請勿使用閃光燈　No Flash

愛護草坪，足下留情　Keep Off The Grass

請愛護公共設施　Take Care Of Public Property

旅遊紀念品商店　Souvenir Shop

未經允許，不準停車　Assigned Parking Only

禁止擺賣　No Venders.

禁止跨越護欄　No Climbing Over The Fence

旅遊度假區　Vacation Resort

度假村　Holiday Resort

便民服務站　Service Center

休閒中心　Leisure Center

老年旅行服務中心　Tourist Center For Senior Citizens

錄像廳　Video Room

車入區　Drive-In Area

步入區　Pedestrian Area

觀纜車　Cable Car

需要幫助，請按按鈕/請按鈴　Press / Ring For Assistance

遊客問訊處　Visitors Info

野生動物觀賞區　Wildlife Viewing Area

景區一日遊　A Day-Long Scenic Tour

北京七日遊　A Week's Trip To Beijing

自行車租賃　Bicycle Rental

小心臺階間跨度　Mind The Gap

僅作火警安全出口　Fire Exit Only

請勿在此倒垃圾　No Littering

謝絕外來食物飲料　No Outside Food Or Beverage

非本園車輛禁止入內　Authorized Vehicles Only

免費上網　Free Internet Access

公園入口　Park Entrance

售票口/ 購票處　Ticket Office / Booking Office

驗票處　Ticket Check / Ticket Collection / Admittance

購票須知　Booking / Ticketing Information

兒童與老人免費　Free Admission For Children And Seniors

6 歲以下兒童免費　Free To Children Aged Under 6

成人年卡（18 周歲以上成人）　Annual Card（For Adults Aged 18 And Above）

一米以上兒童需每人一票　Children Taller Than 1 Meter Must Pay

Full Fare

購票中請當面清點票款，門票售出，恕不退款　Check The Change Before You Leave / No Refund For Tickets Sold

遊客必須每人持票入內，廢票、偽造票不得入內　Admission By Valid Tickets Only

70周歲以上老人、退休人員、殘疾人憑相關有效證件入場　Valid ID Admission For Seniors Over 70, Retired Veteran Cadres AndThe Disabled

暫停服務請諒解　Temporarily Closed. Sorry For The Inconvenience

六點停止入園　Last Admission：6：00.

閉館／閉場清理時間：早上8～10點　Closed For Cleaning：8：00-10：00 am

　　遊客中心　Tourist Center

　　旅遊地圖　Tourist Maps

　　醫務室　Clinic

　　無烟餐廳　Non-Smoking Restaurant

　　快餐　Snack Bar

　　商店　Shop

　　酒吧　Bar / Pub

　　請付現金　Please Pay In Cash

　　廁所　Toilet

　　導遊服務　Tour Guide Service

　　照相服務　Photo Service

　　郵政服務　Postal Service

　　公用電話　Public Phone / Phone

　　小件寄存　Left Luggage

遊客投訴電話　Tourist Complaint Phone

遊客諮詢電話　Tourist Information Phone

禁止吸烟　No Smoking

禁止遊泳　No Swimming

此處嚴禁垂釣　No Fishing Here

禁止踐踏草坪　Please Keep Off The Lawn

請勿攀折花木　Please Don't Pick The Flowers

禁放風箏　No Kite Flying

禁止餵食　No Feeding

勿近水塘　Stay Off Pond

水深危險　Deep Water

安全須知　Safety Instructions

自行車出租　Cycle / Bicycle Hire

前臺　Front Desk

穿好救生衣　Life Jacket Required

兒童要有成人陪同　Children Must Be Accompanied By An Adult

觀光走廊　Viewing Gallery

動物觀賞區　Animal Viewing Area

禁止寵物入內　No Pets / No Animals Allowed

免費開放　Free Admission / Admission Is Free For All Visitors

請勿進入　Do Not Go Inside

四季旅遊勝地/四季度假勝地　Four Seasons Resort

使用篝火、炭火、便携式火爐，須獲批準　Permit Required: Campfires, Charcoal Fires, Portable Stoves

提供導遊服務　Tour Guides Available

飲料食物，謝絕入內　No Food Or Drink

男廁所　Men's Room（Male）

女廁所　Ladies' Room（Female）

嚴禁煙火　No Open Flames

注意危險，水流湍急　Danger! Strong Currents

4. 文教衛生標識語

教學區　Teaching Area

教師休息室　Teachers' Lounge

教員辦公室　Faculty Office

教室　Classroom

會議室　Meeting Room

學習與電腦實驗室　Learning & Computer Lab

學術報告廳　Lecture Hall

學生工作處　Students Affairs Office

學生中心　Student Center

學生會　Student Union

學生管理大樓　Student Administration Building

註冊處　Registration Office

語音室　Language Lab

電腦室　Computer Lab

廣播站　Broadcasting Station

影印服務　Photocopy Service

多功能廳　Multipurpose Hall

辦公樓　Office Building / Administration Building

大教室　Lecture Hall

階梯教室　Lecture Theatre
對外聯絡與發展處　Office Of Foreign Liaison & Development
信息辦公室　Information Office
圖書館　Library
資料室　Reference Room
電子閱覽室　E-Reading Room
（圖書館）流通部　Circulation
音樂數位圖書室　Digital Music Library
語音導覽　Audio Guide
中文書刊外借室　Circulation：Books & Periodicals In Chinese
自助閱覽室　Self-service Reading Room
音樂文獻室　Collection Of Musical Documents
請勿喧嘩　No Loud Talk
請保持安靜/禁止喧嘩　Quiet Please
請將手機調整到靜音　Please Silence Cell Phones
不準攜帶食物到圖書館　No Food Allowed
勿帶飲食到教室　No Food Or Drink Permitted In Classrooms
注意歸還日期，按時還書　Return Books In Time
期刊不可外借　Periodicals Are For Library Use Only
超期圖書每冊每天罰款 0.1 元　Library Charges 0.1 Yuan Per Day For Each Overdue Book
話劇藝術中心　Drama Center
劇場休息室　Theater Lobby
入場卡　Admission Card
憑票入場　Admission By Tickets
請妥善保管好您的貴重物品　Take Care Of Your Valuables

觀眾須知　Notice

非本影城出售的食品請勿帶入觀眾廳　No Outside Food Or Drink

導醫　Patient Guide

掛號處　Registration

急診室　Emergency Room

檢驗科　Clinical Laboratory

門診部　Outpatient Department

住院部　Inpatient Department

候診廳　Waiting Lobby

診室　Consulting Room

手術室　Operating Room

注射室　Injection Room

西藥房　Pharmacy

觀察室　Observation Ward

專家門診　Specialists

男士止步　Ladies Only

取報告須知　Lab Report Guide

醫療急救通道　Emergency Passage

需要幫助，請按按鈕　Press For Assistance

婦女、兒童優先　Women And Children First

獻血者召募　Blood Donor Recruitment

中國紅十字會　China Red Cross Society

5. 公益廣告

提高生活質量，邁向美好未來　Better Life, Brighter Future

發展是硬道理　Development Is Of Overriding Importance

成功，源於對高品質的堅持　Success Comes From Unremitting Pursuit Of Quality

全國衛生城市　National Hygienic City

中國歷史名城　A Famous Historic City Of China

全心全意全爲您　Your Needs, Our Priority

地球是我家，清潔靠大家　Let's Keep Our Hometown Clean And Tidy

小草青青，足下留情/愛護綠地，請勿入內/依依芳草，敬請愛憐/請多關愛花草生命/少一個腳印，多一片綠色　Keep Off The Grass

創一流服務，迎四海嘉賓　Best Service For All Our Guests

尊重知識，尊重人才　Respect Knowledge And Talents

請給老年人讓座　Offer Your Seat To The Elderly (Senior)

您的安全，我們的天職　Your Safety Is Our No.1 Concern

警惕烟頭引發火災　Caution! Cigarette Butts Can Cause Fire!

提高人民生活水平　Improve People's Living Standards

地球是我家，綠化靠大家　Keep Our Earth Green

愛心接力代代傳　Pass Love From Generation To Generation

一滴血，一片心，一份愛　Donate Blood To Save Lives

優生優育　Healthy Birth And Sound Care

造福子孫　Benefit Future Generations

做名城市民，講社會公德　Live Up To The Fame Of The City

弘揚體育精神，促進國際往來　Promote Sportsmanship And International Exchanges

發揚社會主義的人道主義精神　Carry Out Socialist Humanitarianism

少了你，我們無法成功　We Can't Spell SUCCESS Without "U"

安全環境大家創，各行各業樂安康　Work For A Safer Environment

健康重於財富　Good Health Is Above Wealth

吸烟有害健康　Smoking Is Harmful To Your Health

知識就是力量　Knowledge Is Power

注意安全，人人有責　Safety Is Everyone's Business / Safety Is Everyone's Job

保護大自然，人人有責　Protecting Nature Is Everyone's Job

心觸一片淨土，愛博一片藍天　Keep The Environment Clean

安全質量，息息相關　Safety And Quality Go Hand In Hand

全面開創社會主義現代化建設的新局面　Open Up An All-Round New Prospect For Socialist Modernization

警惕全球變暖　Global Warming / Global Warning

一個地球，一個家庭　One Earth One Family

只有一個地球——齊關心，共分享　Only One Earth, Care And Share

我們的地球、居住地、家園　Our Earth, Our Habitat, Our Home

拯救地球就是拯救未來　Our Earth—Our Future—Just Save It！

爲了兒童和未來——没有破壞的發展　Only One Future For Our Children—Development Without Destruction

世間萬物 生命之網　Connect With The World Wide Web Of Life

營造綠色城市，呵護地球家園　Green Cities—Plan For The Planet！

第三單元

烹飪及菜名

　　烹飪是膳食的藝術。中國的烹飪，不僅技術精湛，而且自古以來就講究菜肴的美感，注重食物的色、香、味、型。中國菜肴的名稱具有千變萬化、雅俗共賞的特點。中餐菜肴名稱除了根據主、輔、調料及烹飪方法寫實命名以外，還有大量根據歷史典故、神話傳說、名人食趣、菜肴形象着意渲染、引人入勝的命名方式。要將中餐菜名翻譯成英文，就得先瞭解中餐菜名的構成及命名方法。中餐菜名通常由原料名稱，烹制方法，菜肴的色、香、味、形、器，菜肴的創始人或發源地等元素構成。除了這種反應菜肴內容和特色的寫實性命名法，中餐還有很多反應菜肴深刻含義的寫意性命名法。由於漢語和英語兩種語言的巨大差異，我們在翻譯中餐菜名的時候，大多採用寫實性命名法，盡量將菜肴的原料、烹制方法、菜肴的味型等翻譯出來，讓人一目了然。

　　本單元簡單介紹中國菜的分類、中餐常用的烹飪方法和常用調料、中餐菜名翻譯的幾種方法以及常見中餐菜名的翻譯。

一、中國菜的分類 (Classifications of Chinese Cuisine)

1. 八大菜系

中國菜肴在烹飪中有許多流派，其中最有影響和代表性，也爲社會所公認的"八大菜系"（Eight Famous Cuisines）有：

魯菜　Lu Cuisine（Shandong Cuisine）
川菜　Chuan Cuisine（Sichuan Cuisine）
粵菜　Yue Cuisine（Guangdong Cuisine）
閩菜　Min Cuisine（Fujian Cuisine）
蘇菜　Su Cuisine（Jiangsu Cuisine）
浙菜　Zhe Cuisine（Zhejiang Cuisine）
湘菜　Xiang Cuisine（Hunan Cuisine）
徽菜　Hui Cuisine（Anhui Cuisine）

山東菜系（Shandong Cuisine）由濟南和膠東兩部分地方風味組成，味濃厚、嗜蔥蒜，尤以烹制海鮮、湯菜和各種動物內臟爲長。代表菜有德州扒雞 braised chicken Dezhou style，紅燒大蝦 prawns stewed in brown sauce，壇子肉 diced pork in pot，糖醋鯉魚 fried carp with sweet and sour sauce，清湯燕窩羹 bird's nest in a clear soup 等。

四川菜系（Sichuan Cuisine）有成都、重慶兩個流派，以味多、味廣、味厚、味濃著稱。代表菜有魚香肉絲 fried shredded pork with sweet and sour sauce，怪味雞 chicken with special hot sauce，宮保雞丁 spicy diced chicken with peanuts，麻婆豆腐 spicy bean curd，干煸牛肉絲 sauteed beef shreds with chilli 等。

江蘇菜系（Jiangsu Cuisine）由揚州、蘇州、南京地方菜發展而成，其烹調技藝以炖、燜、煨著稱，重視調湯，保持原汁。代表菜有鹽水鴨胗 salted duck gizzards，鬆鼠鱖魚 braised mandarin fish in shape of squirrel，蟹粉魚唇 shark's lip with crabmeat，清湯魚翅 shark's fin in clear soup 等。

浙江菜系（Zhejiang Cuisine）由杭州、寧波、紹興等地方菜構成，最負盛名的是杭州菜。其特點是鮮嫩軟滑，香醇綿糯，清爽不膩。代表菜有西湖醋魚 west lake fish in vinegar gravy，炸響鈴 fried bean-curd skin with meat，龍井蝦仁 stir-fried shrimps with longing tea leaves，咸菜大湯黃魚 braised croaker soup，叫花鷄 beggar's chicken (a whole chicken roasted in a caked mud) 等。

廣東菜系（Guangdong Cuisine）有廣州、潮州、東江三個流派，以廣州菜爲代表，其烹調方法突出煎、炸、燴、炖等，而口味特點是爽、淡、脆、鮮。代表菜有烤乳猪 roast suckling pig，東江鹽焗鷄 salt roasted chicken，白灼基圍蝦 fried greasy back shrimp，燒鵝 roasted goose，蚝油牛肉 fried sliced beef in oyster sauce，沙河粉 rice noodles，艇仔粥 Tingzai porridge 等。

湖南菜系（Hunan Cuisine）由湘江流域、洞庭湖區和湘西山區地方菜發展而成。其特點是注重香辣、麻辣、酸、辣、焦麻、香鮮，尤以酸辣居多。代表菜有紅燒肉 pork braised in brown sauce，東安鷄 Dong'an chicken，臘味合蒸 steamed multiple preserved hams，組庵魚翅 Zuyan shark's fin，冰糖湘蓮 sugar candy lotus 等。

福建菜系（Fujian Cuisine）由福州、泉州、廈門等地方菜系發展而成，並以福州菜爲其代表。其特點是以海味爲主要原料，注重甜酸咸香、色美味鮮。代表菜有鷄湯氽海蚌 braised sea clam with chicken soup，淡糟香螺片 sliced whelk with weak wine sauce，芙蓉鷄丸

steamed chicken ball with egg-white 等。

安徽菜系（Anhui Cuisine）由皖南、沿江和沿淮地方風味構成，皖南菜是主要代表，多以火腿佐味、冰糖提鮮，擅長燒炖，講究火工。代表菜有黄山醉鸽 Huangshan stewed pigeon，無爲熏鴨 Wuwei smoked duck，符離集燒鷄 red-cooked chicken, Fuliji style，石耳炖鷄 stewed hen with stone fungus，鬆仁排骨 crisp pork with pine nuts，绿豆煎餅 green bean pancakes 等。

2. 菜品分類（Types of Courses）

凉菜類　Cold Dishes
熱菜類　Hot Dishes
湯羹粥煲類　Soups, Congees and Casseroles
主食和小吃　Main Food and Snacks

二、常用烹飪方法及調料翻譯

1. 常用烹飪方法

烘烤　bake
煮　boil
用文火炖煮　braise
炸　deep-fry
烤　roast
（直接用火）燒烤　broil

煎　pan-fry
用水煮　poach
爆　quick-fry
燴／炖　stew
嫩煎　sauté
煨　simmer

炒　stir-fry　　　　　　　　　　蒸　steam
加醬汁或成串燒烤　barbecue　　　熏　smoke
腌，用鹵泡　marinate　　　　　　切絲　shred
切片　slice　　　　　　　　　　　搗碎　mash
切成方塊　cube　　　　　　　　　剁碎，切成小塊　chop
切丁　dice

（注意：烹飪方法在翻譯中一般用作修飾語，故英譯時一般用 -ed形式。如：紅燒豬排 stewed pork chop in brown sauce，干炸丸子 deep-fried meat balls，清蒸全鷄 steamed whole chicken in clear soup）

2. 常用烹飪調料

鹽　salt　　　　　　　　　　醬油　soy sauce
醋　vinegar　　　　　　　　味精　monosodium glutamate
澱粉　starch　　　　　　　 芝麻油　sesame oil
植物油　vegetable oil　　　 橄欖油　olive oil
蚝油　oyster oil　　　　　　姜　ginger
葱　green onion　　　　　　蒜　garlic
辣椒　hot（red）pepper　　 胡椒　（black）pepper
芝麻醬　sesame paste　　　 豆豉　salt black bean
料酒　cooking wine　　　　 糖　sugar
鷄精　chicken powder

三、菜名翻譯的幾種方法

1. 以主料爲主，配料或配汁爲輔

(1) 菜肴的主料和配料

主料（名稱/形狀）+ with + 配料。如：

杏仁鷄丁　chicken cubes with almond

番茄炒蛋　scrambled egg with tomato

青椒肉絲　shredded pork and green pepper

(2) 菜肴的主料和配汁

主料 + with /in + 湯汁（sauce）。如：

冰梅涼瓜　bitter melon in plum sauce

蠔油牛肉片　sauté beef slices in oyster sauce

2. 以烹制方法爲主，原料爲輔

(1) 菜肴的做法和主料

做法（動詞過去分詞）+主料（名稱/形狀）。如：

炒鱔片　stir-fried eel slices

軟炸里脊　soft-fried pork fillet

清炖獅子頭　steamed minced pork ball

(2) 菜肴的做法、主料和配料

做法（動詞過去分詞）+主料（名稱/形狀）+配料。如：

豌豆辣牛肉　sautéed spicy beef and green peas

仔姜燒雞條　braised chicken fillet with tender ginger

（3）菜肴的做法、主料和湯汁

做法（動詞過去分詞）+ 主料（名稱/形狀）+ with ／ in + 湯汁。如：

川北涼粉　tossed clear noodles with chili sauce

魚香肉絲　fried shredded pork with sweet and sour sauce

清炖猪蹄　stewed pig hoof in clean soup

3. 以形狀、口感爲主，原料爲輔

（1）菜肴形狀或口感以及主配料

形狀/口感 + 主料。如：

玉兔饅頭　rabbit-shaped Mantou

脆皮鷄　crispy chicken

（2）菜肴的做法、形狀或口感、做法以及主配料

做法（動詞過去分詞）+ 形狀/口感 + 主料 + 配料。如：

宮爆肉丁　stir-fried diced pork with chili ／ chili sauce and peanuts

茄汁燴魚片　stewed fish slices with tomato sauce

4. 以人名、地名爲主，原料爲輔

（1）菜肴的創始人（發源地）和主料

人名（地名）+ 主料。如：

麻婆豆腐　Mapo Tofu（sautéed Tofu in hot and spicy sauce）

廣東點心　Cantonese Dim Sum

四川水餃　Sichuan boiled dumpling

（2）菜肴的創始人（發源地）、主配料及做法

做法（動詞過去式）+ 主輔料 + 人名/地名 + style，如：

四川辣子雞　spicy chicken, Sichuan style

北京炸醬麵　noodles with soy bean paste, Beijing style

5. 體現中國餐飲文化，使用漢語拼音命名或音譯

具有中國特色且被外國人接受的傳統食品，本着推廣漢語及中國餐飲文化的原則，使用漢語拼音。

如：餃子 Jiaozi　包子 Baozi　饅頭 Mantou　花卷 Huajuan　燒麥 Shaomai

具有中國特色且已被國外主要英文字典收錄的，使用漢語方言拼寫或音譯拼寫的菜名，仍保留其原拼寫方式。

如：豆腐 Tofu　餛飩 Wonton

6. 中文菜肴名稱無法體現其做法及主配料的，使用漢語拼音，並在後標註英文註釋

如：佛跳牆　Fotiaoqiang（steamed abalone with shark's fin and fish maw in broth）

鍋貼　Guotie（pan-fried dumplings）

油條　Youtiao（deep-fried dough sticks）

湯圓　Tangyuan（glutinous rice balls）

粽子　Zongzi（glutinous rice wrapped in bamboo leaves）

元宵　Yuanxiao（glutinous rice balls for Lantern Festival）

驢打滾兒　Lǘdagunr（glutinous rice rolls stuffed with red bean

paste）

  豆汁兒 Douzhir（fermented bean drink）

  艾窩窩 Aiwowo（steamed rice cakes with sweet stuffing）

四、常見中餐菜名翻譯

1. 菜肴的主料和配料爲主的菜名

  青椒肉絲 shredded pork and green pepper

  腰果蝦仁 fried shrimps with cashew nuts

  辣子鷄丁 sauté pork cubes with chili / hot pepper

  杏仁鷄丁 chicken cubes with almond

  番茄炒蛋 scrambled egg with tomato

  梅干菜扣肉 steamed pork with salted dried mustard cabbage

  咖喱牛肉片 sliced beef in curry sauce

  蒜苗炒猪肝 stir-fried pork liver with garlic sprouts

  番茄炖牛腩 stewed beef brisket with tomato

  栗子紅燒肉 braised pork with chestnuts

  冬笋炒肉絲 sauté shredded pork with bamboo shoots

  芥末拌鴨掌 cold duck webs mixed with mustard

  冬菇菜心 cabbage heart with mushrooms

  冬菇油菜 sauté rape with mushrooms

  鷄茸粟米羹 corn and chicken soup

  尖椒土豆絲 peppers and shredded potatoes

  鷄蛋炒韭菜 sauté eggs with leek

冬菇猪蹄　pig's trotter with mushrooms
肉末青豆　fried green peas with minced pork
蚝油牛肉片　sauté beef slices in oyster sauce
葱頭牛肉絲　shredded beef with onions
桃仁鷄丁　sauté chicken cubes with walnuts
栗子鷄　stewed chicken with chestnuts
茶葉蛋　boiled eggs with tea-leafs
番茄大蝦　prawns with tomato sauce
菠菜豆腐湯　spinach and bean curd soup
番茄鷄蛋湯　tomato and egg soup
肉絲海帶湯　soup of shredded meat with kelps
丸子湯　meat-ball soup
三鮮湯　soup of three delicacies
冬瓜湯　consommé (clear soup) of white gourd
素鷄湯　clear chicken soup
白菜湯　Chinese cabbage soup
肉片湯　sliced pork soup
榨菜肉絲湯　soup with shredded pork and hot pickled mustard greens
酸辣湯　hot and sour soup
黃瓜鷄片湯　soup of cucumber with chicken slices
青豆鷄丁湯　soup of chicken cubes with green peas
蚝油鮑魚　braised abalone with oyster oil
咖喱鷄　chicken in curry sauce
清湯魚肚　consommé (clear soup) of fish maw
茄汁蝦球　fried prawn balls with tomato sauce
蟹肉魚肚　stewed fish maw with crab meat

海米白菜　Chinese cabbage with dried shrimps
菠蘿牛仔骨　stir-fried ox ribs with pineapple
餡餅　pancake with meat fillings / meat-filled pancake
湯麵　noodles with soup / soup noodles

2. 菜肴的主料和烹飪方法爲主的菜名

回鍋肉　twice-cooked pork slices in hot sauce / boiled and fried pork slices

火爆腰花　sautéed pork kidney

軟炸裡脊　soft-fried pork fillet

紅燒肘子　braised (red stewed) pork leg (upper part of pork leg) in brown sauce

紅燒猪排　stewed pork chop in brown sauce

清炖獅子頭　steamed minced pork ball

米粉蒸肉　steamed pork with rice flour

白灼蝦　boiled prawns

熘肝尖　quick-fried liver

醬爆肉（鷄）丁　sauté pork (chicken) cubes with soy paste

白斬鷄　boiled-sliced cold chicken

干炸丸子　deep-fried meat balls

清蒸全鷄（鴨）　steamed whole chicken (duck) in clear soup

宮爆肉丁　stir-fried diced pork with chili / chili sauce and peanuts

鹽煎肉　fried pork with salted pepper

鐵板牛肉　beef steak served on sizzling iron plate

北京烤鴨　roasted Beijing duck

干煸四季豆　fried string beans

醋溜（辣）白菜　starch-coated quick-fried Chinese cabbage with vinegar (hot pepper)

凉拌番茄　sliced tomatoes in sugar salad

凉拌粉皮（絲）　cold sheet jelly (made of bean or potato starch)

鷄油冬笋（扁豆）　sauté bamboo shoots (French beans) in chicken oil

白油烘蛋　baked egg in white oil

口蘑蒸鷄（鴨）　steamed chicken (duck) with truffle (fresh mushrooms)

砂鍋鷄　cooked chicken in casserole

鐵扒牛肉　grilled beef cutlets

清蒸鯉魚　steamed carp

黃酒燜全鴨　braised duck in rice wine

油燜鮮蘑　braised fresh mushrooms

炒裡脊絲　sauté pork fillet shreds

干燒大蝦　fried prawns with hot brown sauce

干燒桂魚　fried mandarin fish with hot brown sauce

紅燒魚翅　braised shark's fin in brown sauce

清炒蝦仁　sauté shrimp meat

燒三鮮　sauté of three delicacies

糟熘魚片　fried fish slices with wine sauce

茄汁燴魚片　stewed fish slices with tomato sauce

干燒黃魚　fried yellow fish with pepper sauce

叉燒肉　grilled pork

葱爆羊肉　stir-fried mutton slices with Chinese onion (green scallion)

紅燒扣肉　braised sliced pork in brown sauce
烤乳猪　roasted sucking pig / roasted baby pig
紅燜肘子　braised pork joint
汽鍋雞　steamed chicken in casserole
鹵水鵝掌　marinated goose webs
紅扒雞（鴨）　braised chicken（duck）in brown sauce
紅燒全雞　stewed whole chicken in brown sauce
炸鴨肝（胗）　deep-fried duck liver（gizzards）
雞絲魚翅　stewed shark's fin with chicken shreds
軟炸大蝦　starch-coated soft-fried prawns
海參燒魚肚　sauté sea cucumber and fish maw
栗子燒白菜　sauté Chinese cabbage with chestnuts
生炒魚片　stir-fried sliced fish
炸雞卷　fried chicken rolls
炸蛋卷　deep-fried egg rolls
冰汁銀耳　white fungus in honey sauce
拔絲蘋果　crisp（rock）sugar-coated apple / toffee apple
拔絲香蕉　crisp（rock）sugar-coated banana / toffee banana
清湯燕窩　consommé of swallow nest
清湯銀耳　consommé of white fungus
糖炒栗子　roasted chestnuts in sugar-coated heated sand
荷葉包鴨　duck wrapped in lotus leaf
酒蒸鴨子　steamed duck with rice wine

3. 主料和味道爲主的菜名

麻辣牛肉　sauté beef with hot pepper and Chinese prickly ash

魚香肉絲　sauté shredded pork in hot sauce / sauté of fish flavored shredded pork

糖醋裡脊　fried pork fillet in sweet and sour sauce

糖醋魚　sweet and sour fish

香辣蟹　sautéed crab in hot and spicy sauce

麻辣豆腐　sauté bean curd with hot pepper and Chinese prickly ash

怪味鷄　multi-flavored（fancy-flavored）chicken

酸甜辣黄瓜條　sweet-sour and chili cucumber slips

椒鹽魚　deep-fried fish served with salt pepper

臭豆腐　preserved smelly bean curd

酸甜菜花　sweet and sour cauliflower

酸辣湯　hot and sour soup

胡辣鷄片　chicken slices with pepper and chili

麻辣海參片　braised sea cucumber with chili / chili sauce

芝麻酥鷄　crisp chicken with sesame

豌豆辣牛肉　sautéed spicy beef and green peas

西湖醋魚　West Lake carp in sweet and sour sauce

咸鴨蛋　sauteed duck egg

4. 形象化的菜名

紅燒獅子頭　Lion's head（deep-fried red-stewed big meat balls in brown sauce）

螞蟻上樹　Ants climbing trees（sauteed vermicelli with spicy minced pork）

夫妻肺片　Fuqi feipian（sliced beef and ox tongue in chili sauce）

木須肉片　sauté pork slices with eggs and fungus

麻婆豆腐　Mapo-doufu / sauté bean curd with minced pork in chili sauce (bean curd invented by a pockmarked woman)

宮保鷄（肉）丁　sauté chicken (pork) cubes with hot pepper and deep-fried crisp peanuts

板栗娃娃菜　sauteed baby cabbage with chestnuts

芙蓉鷄片　chicken slices with eggwhite puffs / sliced chicken in eggwhite sauce

沸騰魚　boiled fish in chili oil

翡翠魚翅　double-boiled shark's fin with vegetable

樟茶鴨　smoked duck

珍珠丸子　meat balls in clear soup

八寶飯　Babaofan (rice pudding with eight-delicious ingredients)

宮保大蝦　sauté prawns with hot sauce

糖葫蘆/冰糖葫蘆　Bingtanghulu (crisp sugar-coated fruit on a stick)

狗不理包子　Goubuli baozi (steamed buns filled with vegetables, meat or other ingredients)

龍虎鬥　battle between dragon and tiger (stir-fried snake and cat's meat)

葫蘆八寶鷄　gourd-shaped chicken with stuffing

黃金玉米　sautéed sweet corn with salted egg yolk

擔擔麵　noodles in chili sauce, Sichuan style

玉兔饅頭　rabbit-shaped Mantou

琵琶大蝦　Pipa shaped deep-fried prawns (Pipa is a Chinese musical instrument)

雙冬扒鴨　stewed duck with mushrooms and bamboo shoots
什錦冷盤　assorted cold dishes
什錦火鍋　mixed meat hot-pot
銀絲卷　steamed rolls (bread) look like silver threads
猫耳朵　cat's ears (steamed cat-ear shaped bread)
大豐收　Dafengshou / big harvest (salad of assorted fresh vegetables)
壽比南山　steamed chicken in pumpkin
驢打滾兒　Lúdagunr (glutinous rice rolls stuffed with red bean paste)
豆腐腦　bean curd jelly served with sauce
豆花兒　condensed bean curd jelly
長壽麵　longevity noodles / long life noodles
黑白菜　sauté Chinese cabbage with black fungus
春卷　Chunjuan / spring rolls
肉龍　steamed rolls with meat inside / steamed meat-filled rolls
鬆花蛋　preserved eggs / limed eggs
腐竹　rolls of dried bean milk creams
油餅　Youbing (deep-fried round and flat dough-cake)
油條　Youtiao (deep-fried twisted long dough sticks)
麻花　Mahua (deep-fried twisted dough, two or three, entangled together, very short and crisp)
餃子　Jiaozi (dumplings / ravioli)
蒸餃　steamed Jiaozi / steamed dumplings (ravioli)
餛飩　Wontun / yuntu (mini jiaozi served in soup)
元宵　Yuanxiao (filled round balls made of glutinous rice-flour for Lantern Festival)
湯圓　Tangyuan (filled balls made of glutinous rice flour and served

with soup)

花卷　steamed rolls

包子　Baozi (steamed buns with fillings of minced vegetables, meat or other ingredients)

玉米/栗面窝头　Wotou (steamed pagoda-shaped bread made of corn flour or chestnut flour / steamed dome-shaped bread made of corn flour)

第四單元
傳統節日及習俗

　　中國傳統節日形式多樣，內容豐富，是中華民族悠久歷史文化的重要組成部分。有這樣一句話："每個民族的傳統節日，反應了這個民族文化最真實的一面。"而中國的傳統節日，正是中華文化的集中展示和民族情感的集中表達。

　　在全球經濟一體化、多元文化不斷交流滲透的今天，伴隨著越來越多的外國節日進入中國爲國人所接受，中國的傳統節日也以其獨有的魅力逐漸被世界各國人民所瞭解和喜愛。

　　準確瞭解中國傳統節日及相關習俗的文化内涵，掌握相關用語的翻譯原則和方案，既可以幫助外國人通過中國傳統節日這個窗口更好地瞭解中國，還可以推動中華文化更好地走向世界。

　　本單元簡單介紹中國主要傳統節日的起源和特點，民俗習慣與慶祝活動的英譯以及二十四節氣的英語表達。本單元最後，我們附上西方主要節日及習俗的英文翻譯供讀者對比學習。

一、中國主要傳統節日及習俗翻譯

1. 春節 Chun Jie（Spring Festival）

春節（Chun Jie／Spring Festival）俗稱"年節"，傳統名稱爲新年、大年、新歲，但口頭上又稱度歲、慶新歲、過年。古時春節曾專指節氣中的立春，也被視爲是一年的開始。在現代，人們把春節定於農曆正月初一，一般至少要到正月十五（上元節）才結束。春節是中華民族最隆重的傳統佳節，也是中國民間最熱鬧的一個傳統節日。在春節期間，中國的漢族和很多少數民族都要舉行各種慶祝活動。這些活動均以祭祀神佛、祭奠祖先、除舊布新、迎喜接福、祈求豐年爲主要內容，帶有濃鬱的民族特色。放鞭炮（set off firecrackers），貼春聯（paste Spring Festival couplets），拜年（pay a New Year call），吃餃子（eat dumplings）是人們慶祝春節的主要習俗。

春節　Chun Jie（Spring Festival）
農曆　lunar calendar
小年　Minor New Year
正月　lunar January（the first month of the lunar calendar）
除夕　New Year's Eve（eve of lunar New Year）
初一　New Year's Day（the first day of the first lunar month）
團圓飯　family reunion dinner
年夜飯　New Year's Eve dinner（the dinner for New Year's Eve）
餃子　Jiaozi／dumpling／Chinese meat ravioli
湯圓　Tangyuan（dumplings made of glutinous rice, rolled into balls

and stuffed with either sweet or spicy fillings）

年糕　glutinous niangao（new year cake）

八寶飯　eight-treasure rice pudding

什錦糖　assorted candies−sweet and fortune

金桔　kumquat−prosperity

蜜冬瓜　candied minter melon−growth and good health

西瓜子　red melon seed−joy, happiness, truth and sincerity

糖蓮子　candied lotus seed−many descendants to come

糖藕　candied lotus root−fulfilling love relationship

紅棗　red dates−prosperity

花生糖　peanut brittle/peanut candy−sweet

春聯　Spring Festival couplets

剪紙　paper-cuts

年畫　New Year paintings

買年貨　special purchases for the Spring Festival / to do Spring Festival shopping

燈籠　lantern

烟花爆竹　fireworks and firecrackers（People scare off evil spirits and ghosts with the loud pop）

紅包　red packets（cash wrapped up in red paper, symbolizing fortune and wealth in the coming year）

舞獅　perform lion dance（The lion is believed to be able to dispel evil and bring good luck）

舞龍　perform dragon dance（to expect good weather and good harvests）

戲曲　traditional Chinese opera

雜耍　vaudeville

燈謎　lantern riddles

燈會　lantern fair

守歲　stay up late or all night on New Year's Eve

中央電視臺春節聯歡晚會　the CCTV New Year's Gala

拜年　pay a New Year call / give New Year's greetings

禁忌　taboo

去晦氣　get rid of the ill-fortune

祭祖宗　offer sacrifices to ancestors

壓歲錢　gift money（yasuiqian，the money used to suppress or put down the evil spirit）

辭舊歲　bid farewell to the old year

掃房　spring cleaning / general house-cleaning

歲歲平安　May you have peace all year round!

出入平安　Safe trip wherever you go

恭喜發財　May you be happy and prosperous! / Wishing you prosperity!

生意興隆　With best wishes for your business!

心想事成　May all your wishes come true!

吉祥如意　Good luck and happiness to you!

金玉滿堂　Treasures fill the home!

國泰民安　May the country be prosperous and the people at peace!

一帆風順　Wish you everything goes well!

祝你新的一年快樂幸福！

Wish you happiness and prosperity in the coming year!

祝你新的一年事業成功，家庭美滿！

Wish you success in your career and happiness of you family in the coming year!

美好的祝願送給你的家庭,新的一年裡闔家歡樂,萬事如意!

A beautiful wish to you and your family—live a happy life and everything goes well in the coming year!

願春節給您帶來新的希望、好運和光明的前程!

May the Spring Festival bring new hope, good luck and bright future!

祝您和您的家人在新的一年裡健康快樂!

May great health and happiness be upon you and your family all the New Year!

願您度過一個吉祥、如意、快樂的新年!

Best wishes for an auspicious, happy and prosperous Chinese New Year!

祝你春節快樂,萬事如意!

Happy New Year! Wishing you a happy and prosperous Spring Festival!

祝來年好運,並取得更大的成就!

Good Luck and great success in the coming new year!

2. 元宵節 Yuanxiao Jie (Lantern Festival)

農曆正月十五元宵節(Yuanxiao Jie / Lantern Festival)),是中國一個重要的傳統節日。正月十五日(the 15th day of the first month of the lunar calendar)是一年中第一個月圓之夜,也是一元復始、大地回春的夜晚,人們對此加以慶祝,是慶賀新春的延續。在古書中,這一天又被稱爲"上元""元夜""元夕"或"元宵",元宵這一名稱一直沿用至今。元宵節是中國漢族和部分兄弟民族的重要傳統節日之一，人們慶祝元宵節的主要活動有：猜燈謎（guess lantern riddles）、耍龍燈（perform dragon lantern dancing）、踩高蹺（walk on stilts）、舞獅子（perform lion dance）、劃旱船（perform land boat dancing）及吃元宵（eat rice glue balls / sweet dumpling）。

  元宵節　Yuanxiao Jie（Lantern Festival）
  元宵　rice glue ball / sweet dumpling
  糯米　glutinous rice
  舞龍/舞獅　perform lion / dragon dance
  猜燈謎　guess lantern riddles
  對對聯　play couplets game
  賞花燈　enjoy beautiful lanterns
  燈會　lantern fair
  耍龍燈　perform dragon lantern dancing
  踩高蹺　walk on stilts
  劃旱船　perform land boat dancing
  扭秧歌　do the yangko dance
  打太平鼓　beat drums while dancing
  腰鼓舞　waist drum dance
  焰火大會　fireworks party
  戲曲　traditional operas
  雜耍　variety show / vaudeville
  元宵廟會　Lantern Festival's temple fair
  彩燈廟會　colored lanterns' temple fair

3. 中秋節 Zhongqiu Jie（Mid-Autumn Day / Mid-Autumn Festival）

　　中秋節（Zhongqiu Jie / Mid-Autumn Day / Mid-Autumn Festival），是中國最重要的傳統節日之一，爲每年農歷八月十五(the 15th day of the 8th month of the lunar calendar)。"中秋"一詞，最早見於《周禮》。根據中國古代歷法，一年有四季，每季三個月，分別被稱爲孟月、仲月、季月，因此秋季的第二月叫仲秋，又因農歷八月十五日，在八月中旬，故稱"中秋"。中秋之夜，月色皎潔，古人把圓月視爲團圓的象徵（a symbol of reunion），因此，又稱八月十五爲"團圓節"。到唐朝初年，中秋節才成爲固定的節日。中秋節一般有吃月餅（eat moon cakes）和賞月（enjoy the full moon）的習俗。中秋節與端午節、春節、清明節並稱爲中國四大傳統節日。

　　中秋節　Mid-Autumn Day / Mid-Autumn Festival
　　月餅　moon cake
　　肉餡/果仁月餅　moon cakes with meat / nuts
　　火腿月餅　ham moon cake
　　柚子　grapefruit / pomelo / shaddock
　　燈籠　lantern / scaldfish
　　嫦娥　Chang'e
　　後羿　Hou Yi
　　嫦娥奔月　Chang'e ascending to the moon
　　賞月　to enjoy the full moon
　　火龍舞　fire dragon dances
　　花好月圓　blooming flowers and full moon

拜月的習俗　the custom of worshipping the moon

家庭團聚/圓　family reunion

慶祝中秋節的習俗　the custom of celebrating Mid-Autumn Festival

4. 端午節 Duanwu Jie（Dragon Boat Festival）

農曆五月初五是端午節（Duanwu Jie / Dragon Boat Festival）。兩千多年來，端午節一直作爲一個多民族全民健身、防疫祛病、避瘟驅毒、祈求健康的民俗佳節。端午節又名端陽節、重午節，據傳是中國古代偉大詩人、世界四大文化名人之一的屈原投汨羅江殉國的日子。爲紀念屈原，便有了每年農曆五月初五的傳統節日。端午節與春節、清明節、中秋節並稱爲中國漢族的四大傳統節日。端午節的主要習俗有：賽龍舟（hold dragon boat race），吃粽子（eat rice dumplings），飲雄黃酒（drink realgar wine），懸艾葉、菖蒲（hang wormwood and calamus），佩香囊（carry spice bag /sachet）等。

端午節　Duanwu Jie（Dragon Boat Festival）

粽子　rice dumplings / Tzung Tzu（a pyramid-shaped dumpling, wrapped in reed leaves with glutinous rice in it）

粽葉　bamboo leaves

艾草　wormwood / artemisia

掛艾草、菖蒲　hang wormwood and calamus

香包　sachet

佩香囊　carry sachet / spice bag

雄黃酒　realgar wine

龍舟　dragon boat

龍舟競賽　dragon boat race

擊鼓　drumbeat

愛國詩人屈原　the patriotic poet Qu Yuan

汨羅江　the Milo River

驅鬼辟邪　to ward off / scare away evil spirits

懸鐘馗像　to hang up the picture of Zhong Kui, the Exorcist

5. 清明節 Qingming Jie (Tomb Sweeping Day)

　　清明節（Qingming Jie / Tomb Sweeping Day）又叫踏青節，是在陽歷的每年4月4日至6日之間，是中國最重要的祭祀節日。唐代詩人杜牧在《清明》中寫到："清明時節雨紛紛，路上行人慾斷魂。借問酒家何處有，牧童遙指杏花村。"寫出了清明節的特殊氣氛。清明節正值春光明媚、草木吐綠，所以古人有清明祭祖（offer sacrifices to ancestors）、踏青（go outing），並開展諸如蕩秋千（swing）、踢蹴鞠（play a game called Cuju）、打馬球（play polo）、放風箏（fly a kite）等一系列體育活動的習俗。

清明節　Qingming Jie (Tomb Sweeping Day)

掃墓　tomb-sweeping

掃墓的人　tomb sweeper

祭祖/上供　offer sacrifices to ancestors

悼文　memorial essay / memorial obituary

踏青　spring outing

放風箏　kite flying

哀悼之情　condolence

紙錢　joss paper / hell note

挽聯　funeral couplet

挽幛　funeral banner
門旁插柳　willow braches inserted on each gate
網上葬禮　online funeral
網上悼念　online tribute
哀悼儀式　mourning ceremony
土葬　inhumation
火葬　cremation
海葬　sea burial
天葬　celestial burial
船棺葬　boat-coffin burial
樹葬　tree burial
花葬　flower burial

6. 七夕節 Qixi Jie（Magpie Festival / Chinese Valentine's Day）

　　每年的農曆七月初七是中國的傳統節日——七夕節（Qixi Jie / Magpie Festival / Chinese Valentine's Day）。七夕節始於中國漢朝，相傳，在每年的這個夜晚，天上的織女與牛郎都要在鵲橋相會。織女是一個美麗聰明、心靈手巧的仙女，凡間的婦女在農曆七月七日夜向織女星乞求智慧和巧藝，也向她求賜美滿姻緣，故稱爲"乞巧"。七夕節是中國的情人節，其主要習俗爲：穿針乞巧（plead for skills by threading a needle）、喜蛛應巧（cobweb as the determinant）、投針驗巧（ingenuity test by floating needle）、拜織女（worship Vega）、拜魁星［worship Kui Xing（the god of literature）］等。

　　七夕節　Qixi Jie（Magpie Festival / Chinese Valentine's Day）
　　乞巧節　Qiqiao Jie（Festival to Plead for Skills）

乞巧　beg for cleverness / needlework skills
穿針乞巧　plead for skills by threading a needle
投針驗巧　ingenuity test by floating needle
喜蛛應巧　cobweb as the determinant
拜織女　worship Vega
拜魁星　worship Kui Xing（the god of literature）
月老廟　matchmaker temple
鵲橋　the bridge of magpies
銀河　the Milky Way / the Heavenly River
織女星　Vega
牛郎星　Altair
民間故事　Chinese folktales
牛郎和織女　Niulang and Zhinv / cowherd and weaving girl
王母娘娘　the Queen of Heaven
玉皇大帝　the Emperor of Heaven / the Supreme Deity of Heaven
天兵天將　heavenly generals and soldiers
天宮　heavenly palace
凡間生活　mundane life
扁擔　shoulder pole
巧食　finger food
八仙桌　square table
刺綉/女紅　needlework
插花　flower arranging
五彩繩　five-colored ropes
供品　offering / sacrifice
花燈　festive lantern / a decorative lantern

宮燈　palace lamp / light
燭臺　candlestick / a candleholder
香爐　incense burner

7. 重陽節　Chongyang Jie（Double Ninth Festival）

　　每年農曆九月九日，爲傳統的重陽節（Chongyang Jie / Double Ninth Festival），又稱"老人節"。因爲《易經》中把"六"定爲陰數，把"九"定爲陽數，九月九日，日月並陽，兩九相重，故而叫重陽，也叫重九。重陽節早在戰國時期就已經形成，到了唐代，重陽被正式定爲民間的節日，此後歷朝歷代沿襲至今。重陽又稱"踏秋"，在這一天所有親人都要一起登高（climb mountains）、賞菊花（enjoy chrysanthemum flowers）、飲菊花酒（drink chrysanthemum wine）、插茱萸（wear dogwood）、吃重陽糕（eat Double Ninth Cake）、放紙鳶（fly a paper crane）。自魏晉起重陽氣氛日漸濃鬱，成爲被歷代文人墨客吟咏最多的幾個傳統節日之一。

　　重陽節　Chongyang Jie（Double Ninth Festival）
　　登高　climb mountains
　　插茱萸　wear dogwood
　　賞菊花　appreciate chrysanthemum flowers
　　飲菊花酒　drink chrysanthemum wine
　　重陽糕　Double Ninth Cake / Chongyang Cake
　　糍粑　ciba / glutinous rice cake（cooked glutinous rice pounded into paste in a stone groove）
　　放紙鳶　fly a paper crane
　　百善孝爲先　Among all the virtues, filial piety is the best

二、中國二十四節氣翻譯（The Twenty-four Solar Terms）

"二十四節氣"（the Twenty-four Solar Terms）是中國人通過觀察太陽周年運動，認知一年中時令、氣候、物候等方面的變化規律所形成的知識體系和社會實踐。中國古人將太陽周年運動軌跡劃分爲24等份，每一份爲一個"節氣"，統稱"二十四節氣"。具體包括：立春、雨水、驚蟄、春分、清明、谷雨、立夏、小滿、芒種、夏至、小暑、大暑、立秋、處暑、白露、秋分、寒露、霜降、立冬、小雪、大雪、冬至、小寒、大寒。"二十四節氣"指導着傳統農業生產和日常生活，一些民間節日習俗也與這些節氣相關。"二十四節氣"是中國傳統曆法體系及其相關實踐活動的重要組成部分。在國際氣象界，這一時間認知體系被譽爲"中國的第五大發明"（the 5th Great Invention of China）。

二十四節氣　the Twenty-four Solar Terms

立春（2月3日或4日）　the Beginning of Spring（1st solar term）

雨水（2月18日或19日）　Rain Water（2nd solar term）

驚蟄（3月5日或6日）　the Waking of Insects（3rd solar term）

春分（3月20日或21日）　the Spring Equinox（4th solar term）

清明（4月5日前後）　Pure Brightness（5th solar term）

谷雨（4月19日或20日）　Grain Rain（6th solar term）

立夏（5月5日或6日）　the Beginning of Summer（7th solar term）

小滿（5月21日前後）　Grain Full（8th solar term）

芒種（6月5日或6日）　Grain in Ear（9th solar term）

夏至（6月21日或22日）　　the Summer Solstice（10th solar term）
小暑（7月7日或8日）　　Slight Heat（11th solar term）
大暑（7月22日或23日）　　Great Heat（12th solar term）
立秋（8月8日前後）　　the beginning of Autumn（13th solar term）
處暑（8月23日前後）　　the Limit of Heat（14th solar term）
白露（9月7日或8日）　　White Dew（15th solar term）
秋分（9月23日前後）　　the Autumnal Equinox（16th solar term）
寒露（10月8日前後）　　Cold Dew（17th solar term）
霜降（10月23日或24日）　　Frost's Descent（18th solar term）
立冬（11月7日或8日）　　the Beginning of Winter（19th solar term）
小雪（11月22日或23日）　　Slight Snow（20th solar term）
大雪（12月7日或8日）　　Great Snow（21st solar term）
冬至（12月22日前後）　　the Winter Solstice（22nd solar term）
小寒（1月5日或6日）　　Minor Cold（23rd solar term）
大寒（1月20日前後）　　Major Cold（24th solar term）

三、西方主要傳統節日及習俗翻譯

1. 聖誕節 Christmas Day（12月25日　December 25th）

聖誕節（Christmas Day）是基督教徒（Christian）紀念耶穌（Jesus Christ）誕生的重要節日。聖誕節從每年的12月24日延續到1月6日。人們在聖誕節到來之前一個月就互贈聖誕卡（Christmas card）等禮物以示祝賀。聖誕節時，街上各店鋪的窗子用紅綠色裝飾起來，與聖誕節有關的商品如雪人、聖誕老人（Santa Claus /

Father Christmas)、牧羊人、天使和耶穌誕生圖等成爲暢銷貨。用杉、鬆、柏等常青樹做成的聖誕樹（Christmas tree）隨處可見。樹上掛有五顏六色的彩燈，各種禮品和彩花，樹頂上還冠有閃閃發光的星星。在聖誕夜（Christmas Eve），孩子們把聖誕襪子（Christmas stocking）掛在壁爐（fireplace）上，第二天早上即可得到聖誕老人的禮物。傳統的聖誕節晚餐有火雞（turkey）、火腿（ham）、甘薯、葡萄干、蜜餞等。

聖誕　the birthday of Jesus Christ

聖誕節　Christmas Day

聖誕頌歌　Christmas carol

聖誕音樂　Christmas music

聖誕卡　Christmas card

聖誕老人　Santa Claus /Father Christmas

聖誕樹　Christmas tree

聖誕夜/聖誕節前夕（12月24日）　Christmas Eve

節禮日（聖誕節的次日）　Boxing Day

聖誕晚會　Christmas party

聖誕節期　Christmas season / Christmastime

聖誕祝賀　Christmas greetings

聖誕採購　Christmas shopping

雪橇　sleigh

馴鹿　reindeer

糖果　candy

烟囱　chimney

壁爐　fireplace

蠟燭　candle

聖誕大餐　Christmas feast / Christmas dinner

耶穌基督　Jesus Christ

聖嬰　Christ Child

聖誕節用的裝飾物品　Christmas ornaments

聖誕節暫停營業、上學、工作期間　Christmas recess

聖誕節假期　Christmas holiday

聖誕郵件　Christmas mails

聖誕舞會　Christmas dance

聖誕布丁　Christmas pudding

聖誕襪　Christmas stockings

烤火雞　roast turkey

銀色聖誕　White Christmas

聖誕快樂！　Merry Christmas！

祝你有個白色的聖誕節！

Wishing you a white Christmas！

祝您在聖誕節所有美夢成真！

Wishing all your wishes come true at Christmas！

在這奇妙的聖誕節，給你最溫暖的祝福！

Warmest wishes for a wonderful Christmas！

祝福您和您的家人聖誕快樂！

Wishing you and your family a very merry Christmas！

聖誕快樂！願聖誕老人帶給你所想要的！

Merry Christmas！Hope Santa bring you what you want！

2. 感恩節 Thanksgiving Day（每年 11 月的第四個星期四　the fourth Thursday of every November）

　　感恩節（Thanksgiving Day）是美國人民的一個盛大節日，也是美國人合家歡聚（family reunion）的節日。每逢感恩節，美國人都要放假 4 天，回家與親人團聚，享受一年之中最講究的一餐──感恩節晚餐。餐桌上有精心烤制、香味撲鼻的烤火雞（roast turkey），周圍用果醬（jam）和南瓜餅（pumpkin pie）陪襯。第一個感恩節是在 1621 年，一批來自歐洲的移民爲感謝上天賜給他們第一個豐收而舉行的慶祝活動，後來延續下來，每年慶祝，但日期並不固定。直到美國獨立後的 1863 年，林肯總統宣布感恩節爲全國性節日。1941 年，美國國會正式將每年 11 月的第四個星期四定爲"感恩節"。感恩節假期一般會從星期四持續到星期天。感恩節過後開業的第一天被稱爲"黑色星期五"（Black Friday），這一天，美國的商場都會推出大量的打折和優惠活動，進行一次大規模的促銷。因美國的商場一般以紅筆記錄赤字，以黑筆記錄盈利，而感恩節後的這個星期五人們瘋狂的搶購使得商場利潤大增，因此被商家們稱作黑色星期五。商家期望通過以這一天開始的聖誕大採購爲這一年獲得最多的盈利。

感恩節　Thanksgiving Day
感恩節快樂　Happy Thanksgiving Day
家人團聚　family reunion
宗教儀式　religious services
黑色星期五　Black Friday
五月花號　Mayflower
清教徒　Puritan

宗教迫害　religious persecution

普利茅斯殖民地　Plymouth Colony

印第安人　Indian

火鷄　Turkey

鹿肉　venison

鵝　goose

紅薯　sweet potatoes

越橘　cranberries

南瓜派　pumpkin pie

祝您和您的家人感恩節快樂！

Wishing you and yours a happy Thanksgiving Day!

深深地感謝您為我所做的一切，感恩節快樂！

Thank you so much for all the things that you have done for me. Have a happy Thanksgiving Day!

祝您感恩節快樂！謝謝您在我需要幫助時伸出援助之手！

Have a nice Thanksgiving Day! Thanks for holding my hand when I needed it!

謝謝你的友誼，祝你過一個美好的感恩節！

Thanks for your friendship. Have a wonderful Thanksgiving Day!

媽媽，您的擁抱和親吻將永遠留在我的心裡，祝您感恩節快樂！

Mom, your hugs and kisses will be stored in my heart each day. Have a happy Thanksgiving Day!

3. 萬聖節前夜 Halloween（10月31日　October 31st）

萬聖節又叫諸聖節，在每年的11月1日，是西方的傳統節日。

而 10 月 31 日萬聖節前夜（Halloween）是這個節日最熱鬧的時刻。在中文裡，常常把萬聖節前夜訛譯為萬聖節（All Saints' Day）。萬聖節前夕是兒童的節日，孩子們徹夜縱情歡樂玩鬧。小孩裝扮成各種可愛的鬼怪逐家逐户地敲門，按響鄰居的門鈴，大叫："Trick or Treat!"（不請客就搗亂）要求獲得糖果，否則就會搗蛋。傳說在這一晚，各種鬼怪也會裝扮成小孩混入大眾之中一起慶祝萬聖節的來臨，而人類為了讓鬼怪感到更融洽才裝扮成各種鬼怪。

萬聖節　Halloween
南瓜　pumpkin
巫婆　witch
巫師　wizard
不給糖，就搗蛋（不招待就使壞）　Trick or Treat!
鬼怪　monster / ghost
杰克燈（空心南瓜燈）　jack-o'-lantern
南瓜燈　pumpkin lantern
咒語　curse
小妖精　goblin
骨頭　bone
掃帚　broomstick
幽靈　ghost
骨頭架　skeleton
面具　mask
蝙蝠　bat
蜘蛛網　spider web
十字架　the cross of Jesus
死神　Grim Reaper

桃木釘　peach nail

僵屍　zombie

吸血鬼　vampire

祝萬聖節快樂！　Happy Halloween

祝你萬聖節充滿不同尋常的魔法！

Hope your Halloween is filled with the night's special magic!

祝你萬聖節快樂！

Just for You, have a nice Halloween!

4. 復活節 Easter（每年春分月圓之後的第一個星期日　the first Sunday after the Spring Equinox and the full moon day of every year）

　　復活節（主復活日）（Easter / Easter Day）是西方一個重要的節日，在每年春分月圓之後的第一個星期日。是慶祝耶穌基督的復活（the resurrection of Jesus Christ），即紀念耶穌基督於公元 30 到 33 年之間被釘死在十字架之後第三天復活的日子。基督徒認為，復活節象徵着重生與希望。鷄蛋是復活節的象徵，它預示着新生命的降臨。節日期間，人們按照傳統習俗把鷄蛋煮熟後塗上紅色，代表耶穌受難後流出的鮮血，也表示復活後的快樂。在多數西方國家，復活節一般要舉行盛大的宗教遊行（Easter Parade）。在復活節的晚上，家人團聚，並請來親朋好友一同品嘗各種傳統食品。千百年來，用羊祭祀是基督教徒的古老傳統，而猪象徵着幸運。所以復活節那天，人們把羊肉、熏火腿作為傳統主菜。

　　基督教　Christian

　　耶穌基督　Jesus Christ

復活　resurrection

基督復活　resurrection of Christ

受難　crucifixion

禁食　fasting

祈禱　prayer

懺悔　penance

聖周　Holy Week

復活節三日慶典　Easter Triduum

復活節星期一（復活節的高潮）　Easter Monday

最後的晚餐　Last Supper

十字小面包（復活節的特色面包）　hot cross buns

耶穌受難日（復活節前的星期五）　Good Friday

復活節彩蛋　Easter eggs

尋找復活節彩蛋　Easter egg hunt

放復活節彩蛋的竹籃　Easter basket

最後一個到的是臭雞蛋！　Last one there is a rotten egg!

復活節兔子　Easter Bunny

復活節卡片　Easter card

復活節遊行　Easter parade

願復活節帶給你快樂！

Hope that Easter brings you all the things that make you happy!

願上帝在復活節之時保佑你，時時刻刻保佑你！

May God bless you at Easter, and keep you all year through!

5. 情人節 Valentine's Day（2月14日　February 14th）

情人節（Valentine's Day）又叫聖瓦倫丁節或聖華倫泰節，即每年的 2 月 14 日，是西方的傳統節日之一。這是一個關於愛、浪漫以及花、巧克力、賀卡的具有特殊意義的日子。人們在這一天向自己心儀的人傳遞信息以示愛意（exchange love messages），人們還會組織各種各樣的聚會（social gathering）來慶祝這個特殊的節日，如許多學校舉行情人舞會（ball）。情人節是歐美各國青年人喜愛的節日，且在其他許多國家也開始流行。

約會　date

花束　bunch

玫瑰　rose

巧克力　chocolate

勿忘我　forget-me-not

初戀　puppy love / first love

浪漫的邂逅　cute meet / romantic encounters / romantic moments

墜入愛河　to fall in love

一見鐘情　to fall in love at the first sight

求婚　propose

情人節卡片　Valentine Cards

燭光晚餐　candlelight dinner

天生一對　a doomed couple

甜心　sweetheart

愛人　lover

愛神丘比特　Cupid

浪漫　romance

激情　heartthrob

誓言　vow

忠心　fidelity

永恒　eternal / immortality

愛情節快樂！　Happy Love Day!

渴望你成爲我的情人！　Eager for you to be my Valentine!

祝你情人節有個好心情！　Wishing You a Happy Heart on V's Day!

和你在一起，每天都是情人節　Everyday is V's Day with you!

爲了你所給予我的幸福、希望、笑容……我將永遠愛你。

I will always love you for what you've given me. The happiness, the hope, the smiles …

第五單元
體育運動

作爲一種特殊的文化現象，體育是跨文化交流的重要手段。當今世界，和平與發展仍是兩大主題，對於加強不同文化背景下人們之間的對話和交流，促進世界和平與發展，體育起着獨特和不可替代的作用。

2016 年，全民健身和健康中國雙雙上升爲國家戰略，與此同時，國家把發展體育產業確定爲穩增長、促發展的重要抓手。體育，不僅作爲文化交流手段，更在個人發展、職業前景、商業機會等方面被賦予了前所未有的想像空間。體育英語從一個概念逐漸發展成爲一門學科，許多行業人士，尤其是大學生對於學習體育英語的熱情日漸高漲。

本單元簡單介紹體育英語詞彙的構成特點，體育運動一般用語及表達，世界大型體育運動會、國內外專項體育組織機構名稱以及世界主要體育賽事名稱的翻譯。

一、體育英語詞彙的構成

體育英語詞彙與其他專業詞彙一樣，有着自身的發展規律及特點。體育英語詞彙的構成一般有以下幾種類型：

1. 縮寫詞

　　為了便於記憶和表達，體育英語中使用了大量的縮略詞。用得較多的一類縮略詞是由詞組中每個單詞的首字母大寫組合而成的新詞，這類詞多用來表示國家、體育協會或組織的名稱。如：

　　USA（United States of America 美國），NBA（National Basketball Association 美國職業籃球賽），UEFA（Union of European Football Association 歐洲足聯），IOC（the International Olympic Committee 國際奧委會），CUBA（Chinese University Basketball Association 中國大學生籃球聯賽）等。

2. 合成詞

　　合成詞是指由兩個或兩個以上的詞，組合在一起而構成的新詞。合成詞是體育英語詞彙另一種常見構詞形式，在體育英語中應用得最為廣泛，表示的內容也是多方面的。如：

　　record breaker（紀錄創造者），record holder（紀錄保持者），free kick（任意球），goal keeper（守門員），gold medal（金牌），alpine skiing（高山滑雪）等。

3. 加綴詞

　　加綴詞是指在詞根的基礎上通過加前綴或後綴而構成的新詞，它為體育英語補充了大量的詞彙。這一新詞的詞意也就在原詞根的基礎上向外擴展或將原詞根的詞意細化。如：

　　substitute（替補球員），quarterfinals（四分之一決賽），semifinals（半決賽）等。

4. 外來詞

　　有些體育項目的術語具有鮮明的民族個性或地方特色，因此，直接採用這些外來語名稱，更能體現這些運動項目的本源，讓人瞭解其背後的歷史。如：

　　Taijiquan（太極拳，源於中國），Taekwondo（跆拳道，源於朝鮮半島），Yoga（瑜伽，源於印度），Judo（柔道，源於日本）等。

5. 新詞

　　體育運動的迅猛發展帶動了體育新詞的產生。如：

　　Hot Yoga（高溫瑜伽），Parkour（跑酷），Plank（平板支撐）等。

二、體育運動一般用語翻譯

　　　　球類運動　　ball games
　　　　田徑運動　　track and field / athletics
　　　　水上運動　　aquatic sports
　　　　冰上運動　　ice sports
　　　　室內運動　　indoor sports

夏季運動　summer sports

冬季運動　winter sports

運動員　athlete

運動健將　master of sports

參加比賽的運動員　contestant / competitor

老將　veteran

業餘運動員　amateur

世界名選手　world-famous athlete

種子選手　seeded player / seed

優秀選手　topnotch athlete / top-ranking athlete

後起之秀　up-and-coming athlete

新手　beginner

替補隊員　substitute

領隊　team leader

隊長　captain

場上隊長　playing captain

教練員　coach / trainer

主隊　home team

客隊　visiting team

種子隊　seeded team

國家隊　national team

省（市）代表隊　provincial (municipal) team

對手　opponent

裁判員　referee / judge

記分員　scorekeeper

發令員　starter

計時員　timekeeper
運動會　sports meet / athletic meeting / games
東道國　host nation
比賽　contest / competition / tournament
國際比賽　international tournament
邀請賽　invitational（invitation）tournament
選拔賽　tryouts
錦標賽　championship
團體賽　team competition
聯賽　league
（一場）比賽　match
表演賽　exhibition match
友誼賽　friendly match
淘汰賽　elimination
循環賽　round robin
小組循環賽　group round robin
對抗賽　dual meet
團隊項目　team event
單項　individual event
男子項目　men's event
女子項目　women's event
預賽　preliminary trials
四分之一決賽　quarter-finals
復賽/半決賽　semi-finals
決賽　finals
體育場　sports field / sports ground / stadium

體育館　gymnasium / gym / indoor stadium

體育中心　sports center

觀眾看臺　stands

觀眾　spectator

運動愛好者　sports fan / sports enthusiast

體育道德　sportsmanship

友誼第一，比賽第二　Friendship first, competition second

勝不驕，敗不餒　Don't be dizzy with success, nor discouraged by failure

為祖國爭光　win honors for the motherland

三、世界大型體育運動會翻譯

奧林匹克運動會 Olympic Games

奧林匹克運動會（Olympic Games）簡稱"奧運會"，是國際奧林匹克委員會（IOC，the International Olympic Committee）主辦的世界規模最大的綜合性運動會，每四年舉辦一屆，會期不超過16日，分為夏季奧運會（夏奧運 Summer Olympic Games）、冬季奧運會（冬奧會 Winter Olympic Games）、夏季殘疾人奧運會（殘奧會 Paralympic Games）、冬季殘疾人奧運會、夏季青年奧運會（青奧會 Youth Olympic Games）和冬季青年奧運會。

奧林匹克運動會發源於兩千多年前的古希臘，因舉辦地在奧林匹亞而得名。在古代奧林匹克運動會停辦了1 500年之後，法國人顧拜旦於19世紀末提出舉辦現代奧林匹克運動會的倡議。1894年國際奧林匹克委員會成立，1896年舉辦了首屆夏季奧運會，1960年舉辦了首屆殘奧會，2010年舉辦了首屆青奧會。現任國際奧委會主席（President of the IOC）是德國人托馬斯‧巴赫（Thomas Bach）。

奧林匹克精神　Olympic spirit
奧運會會歌　Olympic anthem
奧運會會徽　Olympic emblem
奧林匹克五環　Olympic Rings
奧林匹克憲章　Olympic Charter
奧運會會旗　Olympic flag
奧運會吉祥物　Olympic mascot
奧運會紀錄　Olympic record
奧運會口號　Olympic motto
奧運會年　Olympic Year
奧運會聖火　Olympic flame
奧運會誓詞　Olympic oath
奧運會項目　Olympic events
奧運會選手　Olympians
殘奧會　Paralympic Games
夏奧會　Summer Olympic Games
冬奧會　Winter Olympic Games
申辦城市　the bidding city
主辦城市　the host city
協辦城市　the co-host city
候選城市　the candidate city
奧運場館　Olympic venues
奧運村　Olympic village

奧運火炬　Olympic torch

火炬傳遞　the torch relay

火炬傳遞主題　the theme of torch relay

火炬點燃儀式　the torch lighting ceremony

火炬手　torch bearer

護跑手　escort runner

起跑儀式　launching ceremony

聖火交接儀式　flame handover ceremony

聖火盆　cauldron

奧林匹克聖火和火炬接力的神聖感、純潔性和唯一性　the sanctity, purity and exclusiveness integral to the Olympic Flame and the Olympic Torch Relay

開幕式　opening ceremony

閉幕式　closing ceremony

頒獎儀式　awarding ceremony

升國旗、奏國歌　raise national flag and play national anthem

頒獎臺　podium

金牌　gold medal

銀牌　silver medal

銅牌　bronze medal

金牌得主　gold medalist

銀牌得主　silver medalist

銅牌得主　bronze medalist

記錄創造者　record breaker

紀錄保持者　record holder

體育道德　sportsmanship / promotion of ethics in sports

藥檢　drug test

更快，更高，更強　Faster, Higher, Stronger（Citius, Altius, Fortius）

顧拜旦（現代奧運之父）　Baron Pierre de Coubertin

國際奧委會　International Olympic Committee（IOC）

國際奧委會主席　President of the IOC

奧運會 28 項運動項目　The 28 events of Olympic Games

田徑　Athletics

棒球　Baseball

壘球　Softball

帆船帆板　Sailing

舉重　Weightlifting

擊劍　Fencing

籃球　Basketball

排球（含沙灘排球）　Volleyball（including Beach Volleyball）

足球　Football

馬術　Equestrian

乒乓球　Table Tennis

拳擊　Boxing

柔道　Judo

賽艇　Rowing

射擊　Shooting

皮劃艇激流回旋　Canoe / Kayak-Slalom

射箭　Archery

手球　Handball

摔跤　Wrestling

水上運動（遊泳、跳水、花樣遊泳、水球） Aquatic Sports (Swimming, Diving, Synchronized Swimming, Water Polo)

跆拳道　Taekwondo

體操（競技體操、藝術體操） Gymnastics (Artistic Gymnastics, Rhythmic Gymnastics)

鐵人三項　Triathlon

網球　Tennis

現代五項　Modern Pentathlon

羽毛球　Badminton

自行車　Cycling

曲棍球　Hockey

2. 世界大學生運動會　World University Games / Universiade

世界大學生運動會（World University Games 或 Universiade），U-niversiade 由 University 和 Olympiad（奧林匹克運動會）兩個單詞組合而成，意爲"大學生運動會"。世界大學生運動會，素有"小奧運會"之稱，由"國際大學生體育聯合會"（International University Sports Federation）主辦，是只限在校大學生和畢業不超過兩年的大學生（年齡限制爲17~28歲）參加的世界大型綜合性運動會。現在世界大學生運動會分夏季世界大學生運動會及冬季世界大學生運動會，皆爲每兩年舉行一次。

3. 亞運會　Asian Games

亞洲運動會（Asian Games）簡稱亞運會。主要在亞洲地區舉行，是亞洲規模最大的綜合性運動會，由亞洲奧林匹克理事會（Olympic Council of Asia）主辦，每四年舉辦一屆，與奧林匹克運動會相間舉行。參與國主要分布在東亞、東南亞、南亞、中亞，包括中國、日本、韓國、文萊、馬來西亞、菲律賓、印度、斯裡蘭卡等國。亞運會的比賽項目有：射箭（Archery）、田徑（Athletics）、羽毛球（Badminton）、棒球（Baseball）、籃球（Basketball）、臺球（Billiard Ball）、保齡球（Bowling）、拳擊（Boxing）、皮劃艇（Canoe/Kayak）、自行車（Cycling）、馬術（Equestrian）、擊劍（Fencing）、足球（Football）、高爾夫球（Golf Ball）、體操（含藝術體操、蹦床）[Gymnastics（including Rhythmic Gymnastics，Trampoline）]、手球（handball）、曲棍球（Hockey）、柔道（Judo）、卡巴迪（Kabaddi）、空手道（Karate）、現代五項（Modern Pentathlon）、賽艇（Rowing）、橄欖球（Rugby）、藤球（Sepak Takraw）、射擊（Shooting）、軟式網球（Soft Tennis）、壘球（Softball）、壁球（Squash）、遊泳（含花樣遊泳、跳水和水球）[Swimming（including Synchronized Swimming，Diving，Water Polo）]、乒乓球（TableTennis）、跆拳道（Taekwondo）、網球（Tennis）、排球（含沙灘排球）[Volleyball（including Beach Volleyball）]、舉重（Weightlifting）、摔跤（Wrestling）、武術（Wushu，Chinese Martial Arts）、帆船（Sailing）、鐵人三項（Triathlon）。

四、國內外專項體育組織名稱翻譯

　　國家體育總局　General Administration of Sports
　　中華全國體育總會　All-China Sports Federation

中國奧林匹克委員會　Chinese Olympic Committee
體育設施標準管理辦公室　Sports Facilities Standard Authority
中國籃球協會　Chinese Basketball Association
中國排球協會　Chinese Volleyball Association
中國乒乓球協會　Chinese Table Tennis Association
中國拳擊協會　Chinese Boxing Association
中國柔道協會　Chinese Judo Association
中國田徑協會　Chinese Athletics Association
中國網球協會　Chinese Tennis Association
中國遊泳協會　Chinese Swimming Association
中國羽毛球協會　Chinese Badminton Association
中國自行車協會　Chinese Cycling Association
中國足球協會　Chinese Football Association
中國橋牌協會　Chinese Bridge Association
中國武術協會　Chinese Wushu Association
中國滑冰協會　Chinese Skating Association
中國健美操協會　Chinese Aerobic Association
國際體操聯合會　International Federation of Gymnastics（FIG）
國際田徑聯合會　International Association of Athletics Federations（IAAF）
國際鐵人三項聯盟　International Triathlon Union（ITU）
國際網球聯合會　International Tennis Federation（ITF）
國際現代五項聯盟　Union Internationale de Pentathlon Moderne（UIPM）／International Union of Modern Pentathlon
國際遊泳聯合會　Fédération Internationale de Natation Association（FINA）／International Swimming Federation

國際羽毛球聯合會　International Badminton Federation（IBF）

　　　國際自行車聯盟　Union Cycliste International（UCI）

　　　國際足球聯合會　Fédération Internationale de Football Association（FIFA）／International Football Federation

　　　國際籃球聯合會　Fédération Internationale de Basketball（FIBA）／International Basketball Federation

　　　國際棒球聯合會　International Baseball Federation（IBAF）

　　　國際帆船聯合會　International Sailing Federation（ISAF）

　　　國際擊劍聯合會　Federation Internationale d'Escime（FIE）

　　　國際舉重聯合會　International Weightliftingé Federation（IWF）

　　　國際壘球聯合會　International Softball Federation（ISF）

　　　國際馬術聯合會　Fédération Equestre Internationale（FEI）／International Equestrian Federation

　　　國際皮劃艇聯合會　International Canoe Federation（ICF）

　　　國際排球聯合會　Federation Internationale de Volleyball（FIVB）

　　　國際乒乓球聯合會　International Table Tennis Federation（ITTF）

　　　國際曲棍球聯合會　International Hockey Federation（FIH）

　　　國際柔道聯合會　International Judo Federation（IJF）

　　　國際賽艇聯合會　Federation Internationale des Sociétés d'Aviron（FISA）／International Rowing Federation

　　　國際射擊運動聯合會　International Shooting Sports Federation（ISSF）

　　　國際射箭聯合會　International Archery Federation（FITA）

　　　國際拳擊聯合會　International Boxing Federation（IBF）

　　　國際手球聯合會　International Handball Federation（IHF）

　　　國際摔跤聯合會　International Wrestling Federation（FILA）

五、世界主要體育賽事名稱翻譯

當今世界重要錦標賽有：

世界田徑錦標賽 World Athletics Championships；世界籃球錦標賽 World Basketball Championships；世界排球錦標賽 World Volleyball Championships；世界體操錦標賽 World Artistic Gymnastics Championships；世界游泳錦標賽 World Swimming Championships；世界乒乓球錦標賽 World Table Tennis Championships；世界羽毛球錦標賽 World Badminton Championships；世界舉重錦標賽 World Weightlifting Championships；世界斯諾克錦標賽 World Snooker Championships；世界射擊錦標賽 World Shooting Championships；世界射箭錦標賽 World Archery Championships；世界跆拳道錦標賽 World Taekwondo Championships；世界武術錦標賽 World Martial Arts Tournament；世界汽車拉力錦標賽 World Rally Championships；世界摩托車錦標賽 World Motorcycle Championships；世界技巧錦標賽 World Skills Championships 等。

溫布爾登網球錦標賽（溫布爾登公開賽） Wimbledon Championship／Wimbledon Open

美國網球公開賽　US Open

法國網球公開賽　French Open

澳大利亞網球公開賽　Austrian Open

世界杯　World Cup

歐洲杯　Euro Cup

歐洲冠軍杯（歐洲冠軍聯賽） UEFA Champions League

聯盟杯　UEFA Cup

英格蘭足球超級聯賽　England Barclays Premiership／Barclays Premier League

英格蘭冠軍聯賽　Football League Championship

英格蘭足總杯　FA Cup（the Football Association Challenge Cup）

義大利足球甲級聯賽　Italy Series A

德國足球甲級聯賽　Germany Series A

西班牙足球甲級聯賽　Spain Series A

法國足球甲級聯賽　Chanpionnat de France de Football

美國男子籃球職業聯賽　National Basketball Association（NBA）

美國女子籃球職業聯賽　Women's National Basketball Association（WNBA）

歐洲籃球錦標賽　FIBA European Basketball Championship

歐洲籃球聯賽　Euroleague（EL）

中國男子籃球職業聯賽　Chinese Basketball Association（CBA）

中國女子籃球聯賽　Women's Chinese Basketball Association（WCBA）

斯坦科維奇洲際籃球冠軍杯賽　Stankovic Continental Champions Cup

美國橄欖球職業聯賽　National Football League（NFL）

北美冰球職業聯賽　National Hockey League（NHL）

北美棒球職業聯賽　Major League Baseball（MLB）

六、熱門體育項目相關表達翻譯

1. 田徑運動（track and field / athletics）

田徑運動　track and field / athletics
田賽　field events
跳高　high jump
跳高運動員　high jumper
背躍式跳高　fosbury flop
撐竿跳高　pole vault
撐竿跳高運動員　pole-vaulter
跳遠　long jump
跳遠運動員　long jumper
三級跳遠　triple jump
三級跳遠運動員　triple jumper
標槍　javelin throw
鉛球　shot put
鐵餅　discus throw
鏈球　hammer throw
沙坑　sandpit / jumping pit
起跳板　take-off board
橫杆　bar
撐杆　vaulting pole
試跳　trial jump

試投　trial throw

徑賽　track events

賽跑　running / race

短距離賽跑　sprint / dash

100（200，400）米賽跑　100m（200m，400m）sprint / dash

中距離賽跑　middle-distance running / race

長跑　long-distance race / distance race

越野賽跑　cross-country race

環城賽跑　round-the-city race

馬拉鬆賽跑　marathon

接力賽跑　relay race

混合接力　medley relay

4×100 米接力　4×100m relay

跨欄賽跑　hurdles / hurdle race

400 米跨欄　400m hurdles

競走項目　walking race

起跑信號　starting signal

"各就各位！"　"On your marks！"

起跑線　starting line（mark）

終點線　finishing line

搶跑　jump the gun

助跑　run-up

發令員　starter

計時員　timekeeper

裁判　judge

裁判長　referee

終點裁判員　judge at the finish

2. 籃球（Basketball）

籃球　basketball
籃球運動員　basketball player
最有價值球員　MVP
籃球場　basketball court
籃板　backboard
籃圈　basket
上半時　first half
下半時　second half
前場　fore court
後場　back court
前鋒　forward
中鋒　centre
後衛　guard
3 分球　three-point shot
3 分線　three-point line
3 秒區　three-second area
近距離投籃　chose-in shot
行進間投籃　action shot / running shot
運球投籃　drive shot
定位投籃　set shot
急停投籃　stop shot
扣籃　dunk shot / over-the rim shot

違例　violation

3 秒違例　3-second violation

帶球走　walking

兩次運球　double dribble

技術犯規　technical foul

侵人犯規　personal foul

打手犯規　hacking foul

帶球撞人　charging with the ball

撞人犯規　charging

阻擋犯規　blocking foul

拉人犯規　grabbing

推人犯規　pushing

雙方犯規　double foul

踢球違例　kicking

走步違例　traveling

全隊犯規　team foul

快攻　quick attack / fast break

混合防守　combined defense

密集防守　bunched defense

人盯人防守　man-for-man（man-to-man）defense

半場緊逼　half-court press

緊逼防守　press defense

被罰下場　foul out

補籃　tip-in

踩線　touch the line

傳球　pass

罰球　free throw

分球　relay a pass

蓋帽　block a shot

神投手　sharpshooter

得分最高球員　top scorer

干擾球　goaltending

攻防轉換　transition

攻擊後衛　shooting guard

組織後衛　point guard

鉤手投籃　hook shot

籃板球　rebound

前場籃板　offensive rebound

後場籃板　defensive rebound

內線隊員　inside man

強側　on-side

弱側　off-side

搶斷　steal

切入　cut

1-1-3 區域聯防　one-one-three zone defense

全場緊逼　all-court press

三人包夾　triple-team

上籃　lay-up

跳球　jump ball

跳投　jump shot

投籃　shoot

投籃命中率　shooting average

外線　outside

運球　dribble

造成對方犯規　draw a foul

擲界外球　throw in

助攻　assist

換人　change of players / substitution

3. 足球（Football / Soccer）

足球　football / soccer

足球場　football field

足球運動員　footballer

352 陣型　3-5-2 formation

433 陣型　4-3-3 formation

442 陣型　4-4-2 formation

中場　midfield

中場隊員　midfielder

守門員　goalkeeper

後衛　back

右（左）後衛　right (left) back

中衛　centre half back

前衛　half back

中前衛　center halfback

右（左）前衛　right (left) half back

前鋒　forward

中鋒　centre forward

右（左）內鋒　inside right（left）forward
右（左）邊鋒　outside right（left）forward
核心球員　key player
絆人犯規　tripping
射門　shoot
近射　close-range shot
遠射　long shot / long drive
勁射　hard shot
補射　tip-in
鏟球　tackle
傳球　pass the ball
接球　take a pass
長傳　long pass
短傳　short pass
直傳　forward pass
橫傳　cross pass
回傳　pass back
斷球　intercept
堵截　block
二過一　wall pass / double pass
單刀　solo drive
倒鈎射門　overhead scissors shot
得分　make a goal
開球　kick-off
角球　corner ball
球門球　goal kick

手觸球　hand ball
頭球　header
任意球　free kick
罰點球　penalty kick
罰球點　penalty kick mark
罰球區　penalty area
點球決勝　penalty shootout
越位　offside
反越位　to beat the offside trap
紅牌　red card
黃牌　yellow card
警告　warning
罰出場　to eject
合理衝撞　fair charge
慣用右腳的　right-footed
慣用左腳的　left-footed
雙腳皆可的　double-footed
前腰　attacking midfielder
後腰　defending midfielder
加時賽　extra period / extra time
假摔　to fake a fall
間接任意球　indirect free kick
金球　golden goal
快速反擊　fast-switching attack
拉人犯規　holding
帽子戲法　hat-trick

球門　goal

球門區　goal area

球門線　goal line

人牆　wall

門框（球門的橫木）　crossbar

球門柱　goalpost

全攻全守足球戰術　total football

傷停補時　stoppage time／injury time

上半時　first half

下半時　second half

腳底停球　trap

推人犯規　pushing

烏龍球　own goal

巡邊員　linesman

延誤比賽　to delay the game

以少打多　to play shorthanded

直接任意球　direct free kick

擲界外球　throw-in

中場休息　half time interval

中圈　kickoff circle

助攻　assist

4. 排球（Volleyball）

排球運動　volleyball

排球運動員　volleyball player

快攻　fast attack

攻擊區/前區　attack area

後區　back zone

死角　dead area

前排隊員　net player

後排隊員　back player

攔網隊員　blocker

扣手/攻手　attacker / spiker

主攻手　ace spiker

過網擊球　over-net hit

後排進攻　back-row attack

觸網　touch the net

攔網　block

發球　serve / service

吊球　drop shot

發球權　right of service

換發球　change of service

跳發球　jump service

助跑發球　running service

發保險球　safe service

二傳　set / set-up

二傳手　setter / passer

接應二傳　wing spiker

背飛　back-flight

封網得分　block point

出界　outside

救球　retrieve / save

扣球　smash / spike / attack

吊球　drop the ball

後排右（一號位）　right back（player No.1）

前排右（二號位）　right forward（player No.2）

技術暫停　technical time-out

快球　fast attack

連擊　double hit

一傳　first pass

自由人　libero

近體快球　quick-A / on-hand spike

平拉開　flat set

空當/無防守區　unprotected area

掩護跳起/晃跳　trick jump

短平快　quick-B

時間差　"time difference" attack / smash after delayed take-off

5. 乒乓球（Table Tennis）

乒乓球　table tennis / paddle

乒乓球運動員　paddler

乒乓球拍　table tennis bat

球臺　table

臺角　corner of the table

臺邊　edge of the table

攻擊性選手　attacking player

防守型選手　defensive player

發球　serve / service

發球不轉　knuckle service

發球得分　service ace

發球搶攻　attack after service

發球失誤　missed service

旋轉發球　spin service

抽球　drive / smash

正手抽球　forehand smash

反手抽球　backhand smash

長球　long shot

短球　short shot

短吊　drop shot

旋轉　spin

削球　chop / slice / cut

搓球　chop over the table / exchange chops

拉球　lift the ball

上旋球　top spin

下旋球　under spin / back spin

側旋球　side spin

弧圈球　loop (drive)

直拍握法　pen-hold grip

橫拍握法　hand-shake grip

擦邊球　edge ball

擦網球　net ball

擦網出界　net out

單打　singles

雙打　doubles

混合雙打　mixed-doubles

扣球　smash

連擊　double hit

兩跳　double bounce

前三板　first three strokes

直線球　straight ball

斜線球　cross ball / diagonal shot

追身球　body hit

長抽短吊　combine long drives with drop shots

近臺快攻　close-to-table fast attack

遠臺防守　far-from-table defense

6. 羽毛球（Badminton）

羽毛球運動　badminton

羽毛球運動員　shuttler

羽毛球　shuttlecock / shuttle

羽毛球拍　badminton racket

單打球場　singles court

雙打球場　doubles court

雙打同伴　partner / pairing

單打、雙打合用的球場　combination court

抽球　drive

吊球　drop

發短球　short service
發高球　high service
發球裁判　service judge
發球過手　service above hand
發球過腰　service above the waist
發球違例　service fault
勾對角　crosscourt flight
換發球　change of service
發球區　service court
失去發球權　hand-out
有發球權　hand-in
回合　rally
擊球　strike
腳違例　foot fault
高手擊球　overhead stroke
低手擊球　underhand stroke
正手扣殺　forehand smash
反手扣殺　backhand smash
球觸網　touch the net
司線員　line judge
滑步　sliding step
擺臂　arm swing
正手握拍法　forehand grip
反手握拍法　backhand grip
蘇迪曼杯　Sudirman Cup
湯姆斯杯　Thomas Cup

尤伯杯　Uber Cup

7. 網球（Tennis）

網球運動　tennis

網球拍　tennis racket

網球鞋　tennis shoes

觸線球　line ball

底線球　baseline ball

邊線球　sideline ball

直線球　straight ball

底線打法　baseline game

發球區　service area

發球線　service line

雙誤（兩次發球失誤）　double fault

躍起抽球　jump smash

抽低球　low drive

深球　deep ball

重球　heavy ball

高球扣殺　overhead（overhand）smash

一平（網球）　fifteen all

二平（網球）　thirty all

三平（網球）　forty all

15 比 0（網球）　fifteen love

15 平（網球）　fifteen all

零分（網球）　love

0 比 0（網球）　love all
局末平分/平局（網球）　deuce
兩跳　double bounce
ACE 球　ACE
平擊球　flat stroke
破發點　break point
賽點　match point
腳誤　foot fault
霍普曼杯　Hopman Cup
大師杯賽　Tennis Masters Cup
戴維斯杯　Davis Cup

8. 體操（Gymnastics）

體操　gymnastics
體操運動員　gymnast
團體賽　team competition
個人全能比賽　individual all-round competition
個人全能決賽　individual all-round finals
個人單項決賽　individual event finals
單杠　horizontal bar
高低杠　uneven bars
雙杠　parallel bars
跳馬　vaulting horse
鞍馬　pommel horse
吊環　rings

平衡木　balance beam

帶操　ribbon gymnastics

競技體操　artistic gymnastics

自由體操　floor exercise

藝術體操　rhythmic gymnastics

音樂伴奏　music accompaniment

規定動作　compulsory exercises

自選動作　optional（voluntary）exercise

墊上運動　mat exercises

引體向上　pull-up

俯臥撐　push-up

十字支撐　cross

掉下器械　drop off the apparatus

上器械　mount

下器械　dismount

落地　landing

脫手　release grip

結束姿勢　final position

托馬斯全旋　Thomas circle

大回環　giant circle

單臂大回環　single-arm circle

騰躍　vault

羚羊跳　antelope jump

燕式平衡　balance stand

空翻　somersault / salto

前手翻　handspring

後手翻　back handspring
側手翻　cartwheel
起評分　start value
評分　evaluate / evaluation
最低分　lowest mark
最高分　highest mark
滿分　full score
加分　bonus point
扣分　deduct point
難度　difficulty
最後得分　final score

9. 遊泳、跳水（Swimming, Diving）

遊泳　swimming
遊泳選手　swimmer
遊泳池　swimming pool
自由泳　freestyle / crawl stroke
蛙泳　breaststroke
蝶泳　butterfly / butterfly stroke
仰泳　backstroke / back crawl
側泳　sidestroke
蹼泳　fin swimming
遊泳帽　swimming cap
遊泳衣　swimming suit
泳道　lane

泳姿　swimming stroke

換氣　breathing

抽筋　cramp

（腿部）打水　kick

觸邊（壁）　touch the side

護目鏡　swim goggle

個人混合泳　individual medley

混合泳接力　medley relay

馬拉鬆遊泳　marathon swimming

花樣遊泳　synchronized swimming

跳水運動　diving

跳水運動員　diver

跳板跳水　springboard diving

跳臺跳水　platform diving

3 米跳板　three meter springboard

10 米跳臺　ten meter platform

（跳水）自選動作　optional dive / voluntary dive

（跳水）規定動作　required dive

難度系數　degree of difficulty

立定跳水　standing dive

向後跳水　backward dive

向內跳水　inward dive

向前跳水　forward dive

臂立跳水　armstand dive / handstand dive

抱膝跳水　crouched jump

燕式跳水　swallow dive

雙人跳水　synchronized diving

轉體跳水　twist dive

反身跳水　reverse dive

轉體　twist

翻騰　somersault

試跳　trial dive

準備活動（預熱）　warm-up

跑動起跳　running take-off

向前翻騰轉體兩周　forward somersault two twists

（跳水）抱膝　tuck

（跳水）屈體　pike

（跳水）打開　open from pike position

10. 舉重、拳擊（Weightlifting，Boxing）

舉重　weightlifting

舉重運動員　weightlifter

體重級別　weight category

次最輕量級（52 kg 以下）　flyweight

最輕量級（52~56 kg）　bantamweight

次輕量級（56~60 kg）　featherweight

輕量級（60~67.5 kg）　lightweight

中量級（67.5~75 kg）　middleweight

輕重量級（75~82.5 kg）　light heavyweight

次重量級（82.5~90 kg）　middle heavyweight

重量級（90~110 kg）　heavyweight

超重量級（110 kg 以上）　super heavyweight

舉重臺　platform

抓舉　snatch

挺舉　clean and jerk / jerk

走向杠鈴　approach the bar

放下杠鈴　replace the bar

弓箭步　forward lunge

深蹲　deep squat

半蹲　half squat

拳擊運動　boxing

拳擊運動員　boxer

拳擊臺　boxing ring

拳擊手套　boxing glove

拳擊比賽　boxing match

回合　round

擊倒　knock down

擊倒對方使其在規定時間不能起立　knock out

（拳擊中）宣告失敗/判輸　count out

（拳擊）臺上裁判員　referee

11. 武術（Wushu / Martial Arts）

武術　wushu / martial arts

功夫　kung fu

拳術　quanshu / barehanded exercise / Chinese boxing

太極拳　taijiquan / shadow boxing / hexagram boxing

打太極拳　do taijiquan

少林拳　shaolinquan

螳螂拳　mantis boxing

猴拳　monkey boxing

拳法　fist position

指法　finger position

掌法　palm position

腿法　leg position

平衡練習　balancing exercise

提膝平衡　balance with one knee raised

基本姿勢　basic position

屈膝　bending of knee

弓腿　bending of leg

馬步　horse stance

弓步　bow stance

坐盤　sitting stance

與眼平　at eye level

與鼻平　at nose level

收腹　draw the abdomen in

收臀　keep buttocks pulled in

兩肘鬆垂　keep elbows loose and downward

前掃腿　front sweep

後掃腿　back sweep

劈叉　split

上體左轉　turn trunk to the left

重心移至右腿　shift weight on to right leg

實步　solid step

虛步　empty step

12. 鐵人三項（Triathlon）

鐵人三項運動起源於美國，是體育運動項目之一，屬於新興綜合性運動競賽項目。比賽由天然水域遊泳、公路自行車、公路長跑按順序組成，運動員需要一鼓作氣賽完全程。2000 年成為奧運會項目，2006 年成為亞運會項目。

鐵人三項運動　triathlon

10 公里賽跑　10-kilometer run

1 500 米遊泳　1 500-meter swim

40 公里自行車賽　40-kilometer bicycle race

13. 現代五項（Modern Pentathlon）

現代五項是由"現代奧林匹克之父"顧拜旦先生發起創立的項目，這項運動起源於法國拿破侖時代的陸軍單兵戰鬥技能，經改進後在大約一個世紀前進入奧運會。現代五項是一種包含射擊、擊劍、遊泳、馬術和跑步的多項目運動。

現代五項運動　Modern Pentathlon

300 米自由泳遊泳　300-meter freestyle swimming

4 000 米越野跑　4 000-meter cross-country race

馬術　equestrian

手槍射擊　pistol shooting

重劍比賽　epee fencing

第六單元
旅遊景點

　　隨著經濟發展和人們生活水平的提高，旅遊已成爲世界各國人民重要的生活方式，而經濟高速崛起的中國，已然成爲世界第一旅遊大國。據統計，2015 年共有 41.2 億人次國內或出境遊，中國國內旅遊、出境旅遊人次和國內旅遊消費、境外旅遊消費均列世界第一。與此同時，根據世界旅遊組織發布的報告，2015 年到訪中國的國際遊客數量達到 5 690 萬人次，位居全球第四。

　　在中國旅遊業高速發展的同時，旅遊文化、旅遊管理方面的一些問題也逐漸暴露出來，旅遊景點名稱、相關標識語翻譯不準確、"神翻譯"滿天飛等問題亟待規範提高。

　　高校學生作爲旅遊業發展的生力軍，理應加強學習，爲提高中國旅遊業水平做出應有的貢獻。

　　本單元簡單介紹旅遊景點翻譯的幾種方法，國內各省市著名旅遊景點的翻譯以及一些常見旅遊用語的翻譯，最後我們還附上世界著名景點的翻譯。

一、旅遊景點翻譯的幾種方法

　　旅遊景點名稱翻譯一般有直譯、意譯、音譯、音譯加直譯、直譯加音譯、意譯加直譯等幾種方式。無論採用哪種方法，在翻譯旅遊景點名字時，應盡可能保留風景名勝的特色。

1. 直譯

　　直譯，即逐字翻譯的方法。既保留原名的內容和內涵，又保留原名簡短的語言形式，通順易懂，是一種被廣泛運用於旅遊景點的翻譯方法。如：桃花溪（Peach Blossoms Stream）、迎客鬆（Greeting Pine）、紫竹林（Purple Bamboo Grove）、黑龍潭水庫（Black Dragon Pond Reservoir）、三潭印月（Three Pools Mirroring the Moon）、燕子溝（Swallow Valley）、黃鶴樓（Yellow Crane Tower）等。

2. 意譯

　　翻譯某些有着豐富歷史典故和文化淵源的旅遊景點名稱時，可不拘泥於原名的語言形式，採用意譯方式，進行深層次的理解和翻譯。如養心殿（Hall of Mental Cultivation）、祈年殿（Hall of Prayer for Good Harvests）、頤和園（Summer Palace）、瑤池（Lake of Immortals）、萬年寺（Long life Temple）等。典型例子還有馳名中外的跑馬山，是因當地群衆每年農歷四月初八爲紀念佛祖釋迦牟尼的誕辰在山上舉行賽馬活動，即"四月轉山會"而得名。採用意譯法將"跑馬山"譯爲"Horse-racing Mountain"比音譯法"Paoma Mountain"更通俗易懂，既能讓外國遊客接受，又能有效地傳達出源語信息。

3. 音譯加意譯

　　旅遊景點名稱通常由專名和通名組成。專名是指景點名稱中標識某一特定景觀的獨特名稱，通名是景點的類名稱，如山、河、海、林等。景點作爲地名的一種，基本上都是以詞組或者短語的形式出現，從語法結構上看大多爲專有名稱+種類名稱的偏正詞組形式。在實際運用中，一般採用音意雙譯，即專名音譯，通名意譯的方法。牽涉歷史和傳說中的人物時尤其如此，如茅盾故居（Mao Dun's Former Residence）、杜甫草堂（Dufu's Thatched Cottage）、鄭成功紀念館（Zhengchenggong Museum）等。許多山河湖海的名稱也可採用此譯法，如太湖（Taihu Lake）、黃山（Huangshan Mountain）、華山（Huashan Mountain）、岷江（Minjiang River）等。

4. 音譯加釋義

　　這種方法主要用於富有文化內涵的景點名稱的翻譯。在音譯的基礎上另加釋義，通過括號註釋、同位語（從句）、定語從句等方式對音譯進一步做出解釋。音譯是中外遊客在地名上的一種認同，釋義有助於遊客理解與接受中國文化。如旅遊勝地"九寨溝"因溝內有九個藏寨而得名，因此可以採用音譯加釋義的方法，將之譯爲 Jiuzhaigou（the Ravine of Nine Tibetan Villages）；"花港觀魚"可以譯爲 Hua Gang Guan Yu（Viewing Fish at Flower Harbor）。

二、國內著名旅遊景點翻譯

北京市（Beijing）

天安門廣場及城樓　Tian'anmen Square & Rostrum

故宮博物館/紫禁城　Palace Museum / The Forbidden City

頤和園　Summer Palace

園中園/諧趣園　Garden of Harmonious Interest

祈年殿　Hall of Prayer for Good Harvests

太和殿　Hall of Supreme Harmony

保和殿　Hall of Preserving Harmony

中和殿　Hall of Central Harmony

養心殿　Hall of Mental Cultivation

雍和宮　Yonghegong Lamasery

乾清宮　Palace of Heavenly Purity

圓明園遺址　Ruins of Yuanmingyuan

天壇　Temple of Heaven

地壇　Temple of Earth Park

人民英雄紀念碑　Monument to the People's Heroes

人民大會堂　Great Hall of the People

勞動人民文化宮　Working People's Cultural Palace

革命歷史博物館　Museum of Revolutionary History

中國人民革命軍事博物館　Military Museum of the Chinese People's Revolution

毛主席紀念堂　Chairman Mao Memorial Hall

民族文化宮　the Cultural Palace for Nationalities

中華世紀壇　China Century Altar

北京工人體育館　Beijing Worker's Stadium

首都體育館　Capital Gymnasium

中國美術館　Chinese Art Gallery

中華民族園　Chinese Ethnic Culture Park

北京孔廟　Beijing Confucius Temple

長城　the Great Wall

明十三陵　Ming Tombs

北海公園　Beihai Park

香山公園　Fragrant Hill Park

周口店遺址　Zhoukoudian Ancient Site

天津市（Tianjin）

霍元甲故居　the Former Residence of Huo Yuanjia

曹禺故居　Former Residence of Caoyu

天津媽祖廟　Tianjin Mazu Temple

大沽口炮臺　Dagu Fort Site

民俗大院　Folk Custom Residences

天津古文化街　Tianjin Ancient Cultural Street

奧體中心　Olympic Sports Center

天津東麗湖　Tianjin Dongli Lake

石家大院　Courtyard of Shi Family

天津熱帶植物園　Tianjin Tropical Botanic Garden

楊柳青古鎮　Yangliuqing Ancient Town
楊柳青森林公園　Yangliuqing Forest Park
大悲禪院　Temple of Great Compassion
天津自然博物館　Tianjin Museum of Natural History

黑龍江省（Heilongjiang Province）

哈爾濱　Harbin-The Ice City
太陽島　Sun Island Resort
中央大街步行街　Central Avenue Pedestrian Street
亞布力滑雪場　Yabuli Ski Resort
冰雪世界　Snow and Ice World
五大連池　Five Connected Lakes
鏡泊湖　Jingbo Lake
橫道東北虎林園　Hengdao Tiger Park
俄羅斯風情園　Russian Folk Garden
哈爾濱極地館　The Polar Aquarium of Harbin
漠河北極村　Arctic Pole Village in Mohe

吉林省（Jilin Province）

長白山自然保護區　Changbai Mountain Natural Reserve
長白山天池　Changbai Mountain's Heavenly Lake
長白山溫泉群　Changbaishan Hot Spring Cluster
吉林鬆花湖風景名勝區　Jilin Songhua Lake Scenic Zone
吉林省博物館　Jilin Provincial Museum

長春淨月潭風景名勝區　Changchun Jingyuetan Forest Park

長春電影世紀城　Changchun Movie Wonderland

長春世界雕塑公園　Changchun World Sculpture Park

偽滿皇宮博物館　Puppet Emperor's Palace & Exhibition Hall

向海　Xianghai Natural Reserve

鬆原查干湖　Chagan Lake of Songyuan

通化高句麗古文化遊覽區　Tonghua Gaogouli Ancient Cultural Tourist Zone

向海濕地保護區　Xianghai Wetland Reserve

延邊古長城　the Ancient Great Wall in Yanbian

四平戰役紀念館　Memorial Hall of Siping Campaign

靖宇陵園　Yang Jingyu's Cemetery

遼寧省（Liaoning Province）

沈陽故宮　Shenyang Imperial Palace（a Manchu Version of the Forbidden City）

沈陽世博園　Shenyang International Horticultural Exposition

大連（浪漫之都）　Dalian（A City of Romance）

國家級旅遊度假區——金石灘　National Tourism and Holiday Resort—Jinshitan

國家級風景名勝區——旅順　National Scenery Resort—Lushun

老虎灘極地館　Laohutan Pole Aquarium

聖亞海洋世界　Sunasia Ocean World

珊瑚館　Coral Hall

貝殼館　Shell Museum

本溪水洞　Benxi Water Cave Scenic Spot

鞍山千山（千朵蓮花山）　Qianshan Mountain（Thousand Lotus Mountain）

內蒙古自治區（Inner Mongolian Autonomous Region）

呼和浩特——歷史文化名城　Hohhot City—A Famous Chinese Historical and Cultural City

呼倫貝爾大草原　Hulun Buir Grasslands

成吉思汗陵　Genghis Khan Mausoleum

昭君墓　Zhaojun Tomb（Green "Grave" of "Tmur Urhu"）

呼和浩特五塔寺　Hohhot Five-Pagoda Temple

烏素圖國家森林公園　Wusutu National Forest Park

鄂爾多斯世珍園　Erdos Shizhenyuan

赤峰阿斯哈圖石林景區　Chifeng Asihatu Stone Forest

海拉爾國家森林公園　Hailar National Forest Park

南山生態百亭公園　One-Hundred-Pavilion Ecological Park

呼倫湖　Hunlun Lake

胡楊林沙漠地質公園　Geological Park in Iminqak Desert

河北省（Hebei Province）

革命教育基地——西柏坡　the Famous Site of Revolutionary Education—Xibaipo

承德避暑山莊　Chengde Imperial Mountain Summer Resort

北戴河海濱　Beidaihe Beach

山海關古城牆　Shanhaiguan Ancient Wall

山海關古城　Shanhaiguan Ancient Town

清西陵　Western Qing Mausoleum

清東陵　Eastern Qing Mausoleum

山西省（Shanxi Province）

大同雲岡石窟　Datong Yungang Grottoes

壺口瀑布　Hukou Waterfall

平遙古城　Pingyao Ancient City

晉祠　Memorial Temple of Jin

喬家大院　Qiao Family's Living Quarter

杏花村　Xinghua Vilage

五臺山　Mount Wutai

恒山　Mount Hengshan

八路軍太行紀念館　Taihang Memorial Hall of the Eighth Route Army

陝西省（Shanxi province）

延安寶塔山　Yan'an Pagoda Hill

秦始皇陵　Mausoleum of the First Qin Emperor

秦始皇兵馬俑　Terracotta Army

華清池　Huaqing Hot Spring

黃帝陵　Mausoleum of the Yellow Emperor

阿房宮　Epang Palace

大雁塔　Great Wild Goose Pagoda

小雁塔　Small Wild Goose Pagoda
法門寺　Famen Temple
華山　Mount Huashan
碑林　Forest of Steles
昭陵　Zhaoling Mausoleum
乾陵　Qianling Mausoleum
茂陵　Emperor Wu's Maoling Tomb
鐘樓　Bell Tower
鼓樓　Drum Tower
八路軍西安辦事處紀念館　Memorial Museum of the Eighth Route Army Xi'an Office

甘肅省（Gansu Province）

敦煌莫高窟　Mogao Grotto at Dunhuang / Mogao Caves
敦煌雅丹國家地質公園　Dunhuang Yadan National Geology Park
鳴沙山　Singing Sands Mountain
月牙泉　Crescent Lake
嘉峪關　Jiayuguan Tortress
平涼崆峒山　Pingliang Kongtong Mountain
永靖三門峽黃河景區　Yongjing Yellow River Three Gorges scenic area
甘南大草原　Gannan Plateau Grassland
張掖大佛寺　Zhangye Great Buddhist Temple
麥積山石窟　Maijishan Grottoes

寧夏回族自治區 (Ningxia Huizu Autonomous Region)

西夏王陵　Imperial Tombs of Western Xia
賀蘭山岩畫　Rock Carvings in Helan Mountain
沙湖　Sand Lake
六盤山　Liupan Mountain
水洞溝古人類文化遺址　Ancient Shuidonggou Cultural Relics
銀川南關清真寺　Yinchuan South Gate Mosque
須彌山石窟　Xumi Mountain Grotto
青銅峽108塔　One Hundred and Eight Pagodas in Qingtongxia

新疆維吾爾族自治區 (Xinjiang Uygur Autonomous Region)

吐魯番葡萄溝　Turpan Grape Valley
樓蘭古城　The Ancient City of Loulan
喀納斯湖　Kanas Lake
博斯騰湖　Bosten Lake
坎兒井　Karez Well
火焰山　Flaming Mountain
克孜爾千佛洞　Kezil Thousand-Buddha Grottoes
高昌古城　Gaochang Ancient City
果子溝　Fruit Valley
香妃墓　Apak Hoja Tomb

青海省（Qinghai Province）

青海湖　Qinghai Lake
塔爾寺　Taer Lamasery
文成公主廟　Princess Wencheng Temple
三江源　Source of Three Rivers
勒巴溝岩畫　Lebagou Rock Drawing

四川省（Sichuan Province）

成都錦裡　Jinli Promenade in Chengdu
寬窄巷子　Broad and Narrow Alley
杜甫草堂　Du Fu's Thatched Cottage
武侯祠　Marquis Wu Shrine
文殊院　Wenshu Temple / Monastery
青羊宮　Qingyang Taoist Temple
望江公園　River Viewing Pavilion Park
洛帶客家古鎮　Luodai Hakka Ancient Town
都江堰灌溉系統　Dujiangyan Irrigation System
九寨溝國家公園　Jiuzhaigou National Park
黃龍國家公園　Huanglong National Park
樂山大佛　Leshan Giant Buddha
三星堆考古遺址　Sanxingdui Archaeological Ruins
四川博物館　Sichuan Museum
臥龍國家級自然保護區　Wolong National Nature Reserve

金沙遺址博物館　Jinsha Site Museum

大熊猫繁育研究中心　Giant Panda Breeding Research Center

青城山　Mount Qingcheng

西嶺雪山　Xiling Snow Mountain

峨眉山　Mount Emei

重慶市（Chongqing）

山城夜景　Mountain City Night Scene

解放碑　Jiefangbei's Urban View

洪崖洞　Hongyadong / Hongya Cave

朝天門水景　Chaotianmen's River View

磁器口古鎮　Ciqikou Ancient Town

南北溫泉　South / North Hot Spring

縉雲山　Jinyun Mountain

重慶人民大會堂　Chongqing people's Great Hall

重慶市民族博物館　Chongqing Museum of Ethnography

紅岩村　Hongyan Village

白公館監獄舊址　White Residence Prison Site

渣滓洞集中營　Prison Zhazi

鐵山坪國家森林公園　Tieshanping National Forest Park

老舍故居　Form Residence of Laoshe

大足石刻　Dazu Rock Carvings

金佛山　Jinfo Mountain

長壽湖　Changshou Reservoir

潼南大佛寺　Tongnan Big Buddha Temple

邱少雲烈士紀念館　The Memorial Hall of Qiu Shaoyun
奉節白帝城　Baidi City in Fengjie

西藏自治區（Tibetan Autonomous Region）

布達拉宮　Potala Palace
大昭寺　Jokhang Temple
雅魯藏布大峽谷　Yarlung Zangbo Grand Canyon
昆侖雪山　Kunlung Snow Mountain
藏北羌塘草原　Changtang Grassland
溫泉勝地羊八井　Yangbajing Hot Springs
唐古拉山　Tangula Mountain
天湖納木錯　Lake Namtso

雲南省（Yunnan Province）

世博園景區　The World Horti-Expo Garden
玉龍雪山　Jade Dragon Snow Mountain
麗江城　Ancient Lijiang Town
香格裡拉　Shangri-la
石林景區　Stone Forest Scenic Areas
西雙版納勐侖植物園　Xishuangbanna Menglun Botanical Garden
西雙版納傣族園　Daizu Garden in Xishuangbanna
南詔故都大理　Capital of Nanzhao Kingdom—Dali
騰衝地熱火山　Tengchong Hot Sea Volcano

貴州省（Guizhou Province）

黃果樹瀑布　Huangguoshu Waterfalls
犀牛潭峽谷　Xiniu Pond Gorge
水簾洞　Water Curtain Cavern
龍宮　Dragon Palace
竹海　Bamboo Sea
鳳凰山　Mount Phoenix
梵淨山　Mount Fanjing
茂蘭喀斯特森林　Maolan Karst Forest
咸寧草海　Xianning Grass Sea
遵義會議會址　Zunyi Meeting Site
遵義楊粲墓　Zunyi Yangcan Tomb
安順符文廟　Anshun Fuwen Temple

河南省（Henan Province）

嵩山少林寺　Songshang Shaolin Temple
龍門石窟　Longmen Grottoes
東周王陵　Eastern Zhou Dynasty Imperial Mausoleum
北宋皇陵　Northern Song Dynasty Imperial Mausoleum
洛陽白馬寺　White Horse Temple in Luoyang
開封相國寺　Chancellor Temple in Kaifeng
玄奘故裡　Xuan Zang Former Residence
洛陽太學　Luoyang Imperial College

嵩陽書院　Songyang Academies of Classical Learning

上海市（Shanghai）

上海外灘　The Bund
東方明珠廣播電視塔　the Oriental Pearl Radio & TV Tower
上海城隍廟　City God Temple of Shanghai
豫園　Yu Garden
黃浦江　Huangpu River
外白渡橋　Garden Bridge of Shanghai
上海南京路步行街　Nanjing Road
徐家匯天主教堂　Xujiahui Catholic Church
上海野生動物園　Shanghai Wild Animal Park
東平國家森林公園　Dongping National Forest park
佘山國家森林公園　Sheshan National Forest Park
上海博物館　Shanghai Museum
上海科技館　Shanghai Science and Technology Museum
上海環球金融中心　Shanghai Word Financial Center

安徽省（Anhui Province）

黃山景區　Mt. Huang Scenic Areas
合肥逍遙津　the Leisure Ford in Hefei
合肥明教寺　Mingjiao Temple in Hefei
合肥包公祠　Memorial Temple of Baozheng in Hefei
皖南新四軍紀念館　New fourth Army Memorial Hall in the South

of Anhui

皖南古村落　The Ancient Villages in Southern Anhui Province

山東省（Shandong Province）

泰山景區　Taishan Scenic Areas

青島之旅　Tourism of Qingdao City

古城曲阜　Ancient City—Qufu

孔廟　Confucius Temple

孔林　Living Quarters of the Confucius

蓬萊閣　Penglai Pavilion

浙江省（Zhejiang Province）

杭州西湖　The West Lake in Hangzhou

千島湖　Qiandao Lake

普陀山風景名勝區　The Putuo Mountain Scenic Areas

雁蕩山　Yandang Mountains

靈隱寺　Lingyin Temple

岳飛廟　General Yue Fei's Temple

紹興蘭亭　Lan Pavilion in Shaoxing

魯迅紀念館　Luxun Memorial Hall

蔡元培紀念館　Caiyuanpei Memorial Hall

秋瑾紀念館　Qiujing Memorial Hall

周恩來故居　Zhouenlai Former Residence

杭州宋城　Song Dynasty City in Hangzhou

橫店影視城　Hengdian Movie City

中國茶葉博物館　Chinese Tea Museum

江蘇省（Jiangsu Province）

古都南京　The Ancient Capital—Nanjing City

玄武湖　Xuanwu Lake in Nanjing

莫愁湖　Mou Chou Lake in Nanjing

南京鐘山　Nanjing's Bell Mountain

閱江樓　Viewing River on the Pavilion in Nanjing

清涼山　Qingliang Mountain in Nanjing

北固山　Beigu Mountain in Zhenjiang

金山　Jin Mountain in Zhenjiang

焦山　Jiao Mountain in Zhenjiang

夫子廟　Confucius Temple in Nanjing

中山陵　Dr.Sun Yat-sen's Mausoleum

秦淮河　The Qinhuai River in Nanjing

洪秀全紀念館　Hongxiuquan Memorial Hall in Nanjing

蘇州城　Suzhou City—the Oriental Venice

蘇州園林　Suzhou's Classical Gardens

京杭大運河　the Beijing-Hangzhou Grand Canal

無錫太湖　Taihu Lake in Wuxi

蘇北洪澤湖　Hongze Lake in Northern Jiangsu Province

揚州瘦西湖　Yangzhou's Slim West Lake

常州恐龍園　Dinosaur Garden in Changzhou

江西省（Jiangxi Province）

廬山景區　Mt. Lu Scenic Areas
滕王閣　Tengwang Pavilion
婺源景區　Wuyuan Scenic Areas
石鐘山　Mt.Shizhong Scenic Area
彭澤龍宮洞　Longgong Cave in Pengze County
八一南昌起義紀念館　August 1 Nanchang Uprising Museum
井岡山革命烈士陵園　Revolutionary Martyrs' Mausoleum in Jinggang Mountain
廬山錦繡谷景區　Beautiful Valley Scenic Area in Mt. Lushan

福建省（Fujian Province）

武夷山　Mount Wuyi
鼓浪嶼　Gulangyu—the Garden on the Sea
媽祖廟　Holy Mazu Temple
古田會址　the Site of Glorious Gutian Meeting
濱海火山　Coastal Volcano

湖北省（Hubei Peovince）

黃鶴樓　Yellow Crane Tower
江漢古城　Jianghan Ancient City
武漢古琴臺　Wuhan Guqin Pavilion

秭歸屈原祠　Zigui Qu Yuan Temple

秭歸屈原故裡　Zigui Qu Yuan Former Residence

紀南古城　Jinan Old City

昭君故裡　Zhaojun's Hometown

蒲圻赤壁　Puqi Cliff

長江三峽　Three Gorges over the Yangtze River

三峽大壩　Three Gorges Dam

歸元寺　Guiyuan Temple

九宮山　Mt.Jiugongshan

武當山　Mt.Wudang

神龍架　Mt.Shenlong

二七紀念館　"Twenty-seven" Memorial Hall

武昌起義軍政府舊址　The Former Site of the Wuchang Insurgent Army Government

湖南省（Hunan Province）

南岳衡山　Mount Heng

張家界風景區　Scenic Areas of Zhangjiajie Mountains

岳陽樓　Yueyang Tower

鳳凰古城　Fenghuang Ancient Town

毛澤東故居　Mao Zedong's Former Residence

湖南省博物館　Hunan Provincial Museum

馬王堆漢墓　Han Tombs of Mawangdui

炎帝陵　Emperor Yan's Mausoleum

桃花源　Peach Blossom Garden

南長城　South Great Wall of China

廣東省（Guangdong Province）

孫中山故居　Former Residence of Dr. Sun Yat-sen
錦綉中華　Splendid China
中國民族文化村　Chinese Folk Cultural Village
丹霞山　Danxia Mountain
羅浮山　Luofu Mountain

廣西省（Guangxi Province）

桂林灕江　Lijiang River in Guilin City
陽朔風景區　Yangshuo Scenic Area
象鼻山風景區　Elephant Trunk Hill
北海銀灘　Beihai Silver Beach

海南省（Hainan Province）

海口風景區　Haikou Scenic Areas
三亞之旅　Sanya Tourism
天涯海角　End of the Earth
野波蘿島　Wild Pineapples Island
萬綠園　Evergreen Villages
海口西海岸公園　Haikou Western Coastal Park
海南熱帶海洋世界　Hainan Tropical Oceanic World

亞龍灣　Yalong Bay

居丁珍稀動物園　Juding Zoo of Rare Birds and Animals

萬泉河漂流　Drifting about over the Wanquan River

五指山　The Wuzhishan Mountain

臺灣省（Taiwan）

阿裡山風景區　Alishan Scenic Area

澎湖風景區　Penghu Scenic Area

日月潭風景區　Sun Moon Lake Scenic Area

武陵農場　Wuling Farm

高雄史跡文物陳列館　Gaoxiong Museum of History

萬和宮　Wanhe Temple

五妃廟　Five Concubines Temple

忠烈祠　Revolutionary Martyrs Shrine

五峰旗瀑布　Wufengqi Waterfall

香港（Hong Kong）

中英街　Zhongying Street

新界　New Territories

總督府　Government House

尖沙咀　Tsim Sha Tsui

跑馬地　Happy Valley

香港島　Hong Kong Island

淺水灣　Repulse Bay

維多利亞港　Victoria Harbor
香港迪士尼樂園　Hong Kong Disneyland
香港星光大道　Avenue of Stars, Hong Kong
香港會展中心　Hong Kong Convention and Exhibition Center
大嶼山　Lantau Island

澳門（Macao）

媽祖廟　Mazu Temple / Barra Temple
普濟禪院（觀音堂）　Kun Iam Temple
大炮臺　Monte Fortress
玫瑰聖母堂　St.Dominic's Church
澳門大三巴牌坊　Ruins of St.Paul
澳門博物館　Macao City Museum

三、旅遊相關表達翻譯

1. 旅遊組織機構名稱翻譯

中國青年旅行社　China Youth Travel Agency
中國國際旅行社　China International Travel Agency
國家旅遊局　National Tourism Administration/State Bureau of Tourism
省旅遊局　Provincial Tourism Bureau
市旅遊局　Municipal Tourism Bureau
縣旅遊局　County Tourism Bureau

世界旅遊組織　World Tourism Organization（WTO）

世界旅行社協會聯合會　United Federation of Travel Agents' Associations（UFTAA）

國際酒店協會　International Hotel Association（IHA）

國際民用航空組織　International Civil Aviation Organization（ICAO）

國際航空運輸協會　International Air Transport Association（IATA）

國際旅遊科學專家協會　International Association of Scientific Experts in Tourism（IASET）

國際旅遊學會　International Tourism Studies Association（ITSA）

國際汽車聯合會　International Automobile Federation（IAF）

歐洲旅遊委員會　European Travel Commission（ETC）

國際鐵路聯盟　International Union of Railways（UIC）

國際旅遊聯盟　Alliance Internationale de Tourism（AIT）

婦女旅遊組織國際聯合會　International Federation of Women's Tourism Organization（IFWTO）

國際學生旅遊大會　International Student Travel Conference（ISTC）

國際宿營和旅隊聯合會　International Federation of Camping and Travel Team（IFCTT）

國際旅館與餐館協會組織　International Hotel and Restaurant Association（IHRA）

2. 常用旅遊術語翻譯

旅遊業　tourism trade

旅遊觀光團　tour group / sightseeing party

避暑勝地　summer resort

國家 A 級旅遊風景區　the national A-class tourist spot
自然保護區　natural reserves / national reserves
國家森林公園　national forest park
旅遊度假村　tourist holiday resort
旅店/旅館　hotel / inn
星級酒店　star-related hotel
名勝古跡　scenic spots and historical sights
古城遺址　ruins of an ancient city
人造景觀　artificial scenery
人文景觀　places of historic figures and cultural heritage
民俗村　folk custom park
佛教聖地　Buddha scenic spot
宗教勝地　sacred sites
景點　scenic spot / tourist attraction
風景如畫　picturesque scenery
名山大川　famous mountains and great rivers
壯麗河山　magnificent scenery
佛教名山　famous Buddhist mountains
古建築群　ancient architectural complex
園林建築　garden architecture
古典山水園林　classical landscape garden
山水風光　scenery with mountains and rivers
城市風光　cityscape
湖光山色　landscape of lakes and hills
青山綠水　green hills and clear waters
海濱勝地　seaside resort

海濱浴場　bathing beach
國際旅遊　international tourism
國內遊　home tourism
海上遊　sea journey
乘車遊　bus tour
自駕遊　driving travel
公費遊　public expense tourism / junket
自費遊　tourism at one's own expense / self-financed tour
蜜月遊　honeymoon tour / bridal tour
一日遊　one-day tour / day excursion
周末遊　weekend trip
假日旅遊　holiday travel
登山旅遊　mountaineering tour
春遊　spring outing
夏季旅遊　summer tour
秋遊　autumn outing
冬季遊　winter tour
旅遊計劃　travel program / itinerary
旅遊服務　travel service
導遊　courier / tourist guide
國際導遊　global guide
地陪　local guide
全陪　national guide
兼職導遊　amateur guide
旅行家　veteran traveller
旅遊指南　travel brochure

旅遊紀念品　tourist souvenir

旅遊線路　tourist track / route

旅遊旺季　tourist season / high season

旅遊淡季　slack season of tour

人山人海，人滿爲患　overcrowded / to be packed

中外遊客　tourists from home and abroad

旅伴　travel companion

旅遊用品　travel kit

旅行箱　travelling case

手提旅行包　hold-all bag

旅行袋　travelling bag

睡袋　sleeping bag

旅行折叠床　camp bed for travel

門票　（entrance）ticket

門票費　admission fee

免費景區電子門票　free sightseeing e-coupon

四、世界著名旅遊景點翻譯

亞洲 Asia

喜馬拉雅山　The Himalayas

日本富士山　Mount Fuji, Japan

北海道　Hokkaido, Japan

南山塔　N Seoul Tower, South Korea

印度泰姬陵　Taj Mahal, India

太陽神廟　Konark Sun Temple, India

柬埔寨吳哥窟　Angkor Wat, Cambodia

敏貢佛塔　Mingun Paya, Burma

波德申海灘　Port Dickson Beach, Malaysia

金馬倫高原　Cameron Highlands, Malaysia

安順斜塔　Leaning Tower of Teluk Intan, Malaysia

雙峰塔　Petronas Twin Towers, Malaysia

吉打古堡　Kuala Kedah Fort, Malaysia

印度尼西亞巴厘島　Bali, Indonesia

新加坡聖淘沙島　Sentosa Island, Singapore

亞洲文明博物館　Asian Civilizations Museum, Singapore

泰國北欖鱷魚湖　Crocodile Farm, Thailand

泰國芭堤雅海灘　Pattaya Beach, Thailand

曼谷大皇宮　The Grand palace, Thailand

清邁古城　Chiang Mai Old City, Thailand

曼谷臥佛寺　Temple of the Reclining Buddha, Thailand

普吉島　Phuket Island, Thailand

自由塔　Tower of Freedom, Iran

貝希斯敦銘文　Behistun Inscription, Iran

伊拉克巴比倫遺跡　Babylon, Iraq

麥加　Mecca, Saudi Arabia

土耳其聖索非亞教堂　Mosque of St. Sophia in Istanbul (Constantinople), Turkey

非洲 Africa

肯尼亞内羅畢國家公園　Nairobi National Park, Kenya
撒哈拉大沙漠　Sahara Desert, Sudan
埃及金字塔　Pyramids, Egypt
獅身人面像　The Sphinx, Egypt
底比斯古城及其墓地　Ancient Thebes With Its Necropolis, Egypt
開羅塔　Cairo Tower, Egypt
藍色清真寺　Aqsunqur Mosque, Egypt
白沙漠　White Desert, Egypt
法老村　Pharaonic Village, Egypt
開羅死亡之城　City of the Dead, Egypt
蘇伊士運河　Suez Canal, Egypt
阿斯旺水壩　Aswan High Dam, Egypt
埃及尼羅河　The Nile, Egypt
歷史名城梅克内斯　The Historic City of Meknes, Morocco
青尼羅河瀑布　Blue Nile Falls, Ethiopia
埃塞俄比亞高原　Ethiopian Highlands, Ethiopia
馬賽馬拉國家野生動物保護區　Masai Mara National Reserve, Kenya
索馬裡半島　Somalia Peninsula, Somalia
撒哈拉之眼　Eye of the Sahara, Mauritania
剛果盆地　Congo Basin, Congo
南非大洞　Big Hole, South Africa
南非好望角　Cape of Good Hope, South Africa
十二門徒山　Twelve Apostle, South Africa

南華寺　Nan Hua Temple, South Africa
好望堡　Castle of Good Hope, South Africa
桑給巴爾石頭城　Stone Town of Zanzibar, Tanzania
乞力馬扎羅山　Mount Kilimanjaro, Tanzania
魚河大峽谷　Fish River Canyon, Namibia

大洋洲 Oceania

大堡礁　Great Barrier Reef, Australia
悉尼歌劇院　Sydney Opera House, Australia
袋鼠島　Kangaroo Island, Australia
帝王谷　Kings Canyon, Australia
悉尼皇家植物園　Royal Botanic Gardens, Sydney, Australia
悉尼海港大橋　Sydney Harbor Bridge, Australia
墨爾本唐人街　Chinatown, Melbourne, Australia
聖保羅大教堂　St.Paul's Cathedral, Melbourne, Australia
藍色海洋路　Grand Pacific Drive, Australia
酒杯灣　Wineglass Bay, Australia
木星賭場　Jupiters Casino, Austalia
袋鼠角　Kangaroo Point, Australia
丹翠雨林　Daintree Rainforest, Australia
法蘭士·約瑟夫冰川　Franz Josef Glacier, New Zealand
天空塔　Sky Tower, New Zealand
大教堂廣場　Cathedral Square, New Zealand
奧克蘭碼頭大樓　Auckland Ferry Building, New Zealand
約翰山　Mt. John, New Zealand

皇后鎮聖彼得教堂　Church of St. Peter Queenstown, New Zealand
莫爾斯比港　Port Moresby, Papua New Guinea
庫科早期農業遺址　Kuk Early Agricultural Site, Papua New Guinea
聖誕島　Christmas Island, Kiribati
千禧島　Millennium Island, Kiribati

歐洲 Europe

法國巴黎聖母院　Notre Dame de Paris, France
法國埃菲爾鐵塔　Effiel Tower, France
法國凱旋門　Arch of Triumph, France
法國愛麗舍宮　Elysee Palace, France
法國盧浮宮　Louvre, France
德國科隆大教堂　Kolner Dom, Koln, Germany
義大利比薩斜塔　Leaning Tower of Pisa, Italy
義大利古羅馬圓形劇場　Colosseum in Rome, Italy
希臘巴臺農神廟　Parthenon, Greece
莫斯科紅場　Red Square in Moscow, Russia
伏爾加河　Volga River, Russia
聖彼得堡勝利廣場　Victory Square, Saint Petersburg, Russia
冬宮　Winter Palace, Russia
英國倫敦大笨鐘　Big Ben in London, England
白金漢宮　Buckingham Palace, England
英國海德公園　Hyde Park, England
倫敦塔橋　London Tower Bridge, England
威斯敏斯特大教堂　Westminster Abbey, England

法蘭克福大教堂　Frankfurt Cathedral, Germany

維也納森林　Vienna Woods, Austria

多瑙河　Danube River, Austria

阿爾卑斯山　Alps, Switzerland

瓦倫湖　Walensee, Switzerland

摩洛哥蒙特卡洛　Monte Carlo, Monaco

美洲 The Americas

美國尼亞加拉大瀑布　Niagara Falls, New York State, USA

百慕大　Bermuda, USA

美國夏威夷火奴魯魯　Honolulu, Hawaii, USA

美國黃石國家公園　Yellowstone National Park, USA

美國紐約自由女神像　Statue of Liberty, New York City, USA

美國紐約時代廣場　Times Square, New York City, USA

美國華盛頓白宮　The White House, Washington DC., USA）

美國紐約世界貿易中心　World Trade Center, New York City, USA

美國紐約中央公園　Central Park, New York City, USA

美國約塞米蒂國家公園　Yosemite National Park, USA

美國亞利桑那州大峽谷　Grand Canyon, Arizona, USA

美國加利福尼亞好萊塢　Hollywood, California, USA

加利福尼亞迪士尼樂園　Disneyland, California, USA

美國內華達拉斯維加斯　Las Vegas, Nevada, USA

美國佛羅裡達邁阿密　Miami, Florida, USA

紐約大都會藝術博物館　Metropolitan Museum of Art, New York City, USA

國家槍支博物館　National Firearms Museum, USA
布魯克林大橋　Brooklyn Bridge, New York City, USA
加拿大多倫多　Toronto in Canada—The North Hollywood, Canada
士嘉堡懸崖　Scarborough Bluffs, Canada
尼亞加拉瀑布　Niagara Falls, Canada
多倫多唐人街　Chinatown, Toronto, Canada
喬魯拉大金字塔　Great Pyramid of Cholula, Mexico
太陽金字塔　Pyramid of the Sun, Mexico
月亮金字塔　Pyramid of the Moon, Mexico
墨西哥城鬥牛場　Plaza México, Mexico
巴拿馬大運河　Panama Canal, Panama
伊瓜蘇瀑布　Iguazu Falls, Brazil
亞馬孫河　Amazon River, Brazil
裡約大教堂　Rio de Janeiro Cathedral, Brazil
聖路易斯歷史中心　The Historic Centre of Sao Luis
馬拉卡納體育場　Maracanã Stadium, Brazil
拉普拉塔河-巴拉那河　La Plata Parana River, Argentina
冰川國家公園　Glacier National Park, Argentina
五月廣場　Plaza de Mayo, Argentina

第七單元
證書及職位

近年來，隨著中國對外開放的不斷深入和與世界各國聯繫的不斷加強，越來越多的人走出國門求學和工作，與此同時，來華的外資企業也日益增多。而要在國外考取一個心儀的學校，獲得一份滿意的工作，大多數發往國外的文書均要求附上英文譯文，許多涉外用人單位也要求求職者出示的履歷以及各類證書配上與之相符合的英文。因此，對大學生而言，能夠清楚、準確地翻譯證書和各類考試比賽名稱以及職位名稱十分重要。

本單元簡單介紹證書的特點，幾類與大學生密切相關的證書翻譯範例以及大學生在撰寫出國文書、求職履歷中常常涉及的一些考試和比賽名稱翻譯。爲了方便同學們求職就業，本單元最後，我們還附上一些常見職位名稱的翻譯。

一、證書的特點及翻譯常用句式

證書屬於實用性文體，對用詞和格式有着嚴格的規定，翻譯過程中最重要的是要保證譯文提供的信息準確、真實和可靠。就語言特點而言，中英文證書均具備簡潔、明了、準確的特點。多用專業詞彙或固定的正式結構陳述客觀事實。如中文的"茲證明……""根據/按照/依據"等。相應的英文表達可用"This is to certify that ..."和"based on, in accordance with, hereby"等。就句式而言，證書的句式相對簡單，被動句較常見，不完整句式也會出現。

二、證書翻譯範例

1. 畢業證書

大學畢業證書的正文開頭一般都以校長的身份來證明某某學生準予從該大學畢業（I hereby certify that ...），並附有校長簽名。

畢業證書

學生×××，性別 男，一九九二年五月六日生，二〇一〇年九月至二〇一四年七月在本校能源學院石油工程專業四年制本科就讀，修業期滿，成績合格，準予畢業。

學校印章
××理工大學
校長：
（簽名）

GRADUATION CERTIFICATE

I hereby certify that XXX, male, born on May 6, 1992, was a student of oil engineering major of College of Energy Resources and, having completed the four years' courses from September 2010 to July 2014 and fulfilled all the requirements prescribed by the College, graduated from XX University of Technology in July 2014.

 Seal

(Signature)

President

×× University of Technology

2. 計算機等級考試證書

> 全國計算機等級考試
> 二級合格證書
>
> ×××參加 2008 年 4 月全國計算機等級考試（二級 Visual FoxPro.），成績合格，特發此證。
>
> 證書編號：XXXXXXXXXXXXX
> 身份證號：XXXXXXXXXXXXXXXXX
>
> 教育部考試中心

NATIONAL COMPUTER RANK EXAMINATION CERTIFICATE

 This is to certify that XXX has passed the National Computer Rank Examination and has achieved the following grade:

Grade: 2

Language: Visual FoxPro.

Certificate Number: XXXXXXXXXXXXX

ID Number: XXXXXXXXXXXXXXXXX

National Education Examinations Authority

The Ministry of Education of China

3. 榮譽證書

```
                    獎狀
×××同學：
在 2015-2016 學年度榮獲優秀學生榮譽稱號，特發此獎狀，以資表彰。

                                        ××理工大學
                                        2016 年 7 月 12 日
```

CERTIFICATE OF MERIT

XXX is honored as a model student in the academic year of 2015-2016. This certificate of merit is hereby given in commendation of him.

×× University of Technology
July 12, 2016

三、考試及比賽名稱翻譯

  大學英語四級 CET-4（College English Test-Band 4）
  大學英語六級 CET-6（College English Test-Band 6）
  英語專業四級 TEM-4（Test for English Majors-Band 4）
  英語專業八級 TEM-8（Test for English Majors-Band 8）
  商務英語考試 BEC（Business English Certificate）
  全國英語等級考試 PETS（Public English Test System）
  翻譯專業資格（水平）考試 CATTI（China Accreditation Test for Translators and Interpreters）
  雅思考試 IELTS（International English Language Testing System）
  托福考試 TOEFL（Test of English as a Foreign Language）

全國大學生英語競賽　NECCS（National English Contest for College Students）

"外研社杯"全國英語演講大賽　"FLTRP Cup" English Public Speaking Contest

"21世紀杯"全國英語演講大賽　"21st Century Cup" National English Speech Contest

全國計算機等級考試　NCRE（National Computer Rank Examination）

全國大學生數學建模競賽　China Undergraduate Mathematical Contest in Modeling

全國大學生電子設計競賽　National Undergraduate Electronic Design Contest

亞太大學生機器人大賽　ABU Asia-Pacific Robot Contest / ABU Robocon

全國大學生廣告藝術比賽　National Advertising Art Design Competition for College Students

"挑戰杯"全國大學生創業計劃競賽　"Challenge Cup" National College Student Business Plan Competition

"挑戰杯"全國大學生課外學術科技作品競賽　"Challenge Cup" National College Student Extracurricular Academic Science and Technology Works Competition

ACM國際大學生程序設計競賽　ACM-ICPC/ ICPC（ACM International Collegiate Programming Contest）

全國大學生結構設計競賽　National Structure Design Competition for College Students

全國大學生電子商務"創新、創意、創業"挑戰賽　China National

College Student "Innovation, Originality and Entrepreneurship" Challenge

中國大學生公共關係策劃大賽　China University Students PR Plan Contest

普通話水平測試　National Mandarin（Putonghua） Proficiency Test

英語演講比賽　English Speech Contest

多媒體課件製作大賽　Multimedia Courseware Design Competition

黑板報設計大賽　Blackboard Poster Design Contest

詩歌朗誦比賽　Poetry Recitation Contest

詩歌創作比賽　Poetry Creation Contest

攝影大賽　Photography Competition

足球比賽　Football Match

選美比賽　Beauty Contest

徵文比賽　Essay Competition

話劇比賽　Drama Competition

登山比賽　Mountain-climbing Competition

辯論賽　Debate Competition

網頁設計大賽　Web Page Design Competition

知識風採比賽　Knowledge Competition

軟件設計大賽　Software Design Competition

網站設計競賽　Website Design Competition

畢業設計大賽　Graduation Design Competition

服裝設計大賽　Costume Design Contest

"金話筒"主持人大賽　Golden Microphone Host Competition

實驗技能操作大賽　Experiment Skill and Operation Contest

建築設計競賽　Architectural Design Competition

鋼筆畫比賽　Ink Drawing Contest

節徽設計大賽　Festival Logo Design Contest

博客大賽　Blog Contest

友誼杯籃球賽　Friendship Cup Basketball Match

工程測量比賽　Engineering Survey Competition

大學生科技創新與職業技能競賽　Scientific Innovation and Professional Skills Competition for College Students

女子籃球賽　Women's Basketball Match

高校化學化工實驗技能大賽　College Chemistry and Chemical Experiment Skills Cmpetition

禮儀風采大賽　Manner and Etiquette Contest

班際籃球賽　Inter-class Basketball Match

四、職位名稱翻譯

1. 常見高層職位及英文縮寫

首席執行官　CEO（Chief Executive Officer）

首席財務官　CFO（Chief Finance Officer）

首席運營官　COO（Chief Operation Officer）

首席品牌官　CBO（Chief Brand Officer）

首席文化官　CCO（Chief Cultural Officer）

首席信息官　CIO（Chief Information Officer）

首席知識官　CKO（Chief Knowledge Officer）

首席市場官　CMO（Chief Marketing Officer）

首席談判官　CNO（Chief Negotiation Officer）

藝術總監　CAO（Chief Artistic Officer）

開發總監　CDO（Chief Development Officer）

人力資源總監　CHO（Chief Human Resource Officer）

公關總監　CPO（Chief Public Relation Officer）

質量總監　CQO（Chief Quality Officer）

銷售總監　CSO（Chief Sales Officer）

首席技術官　CTO（Chief Technology Officer）

評估總監　CVO（Chief Valuation Officer）

2. 各類職位名稱翻譯

安保人員　Security Officer / Guard

保潔員　Cleaner

保姆　Nurse

班主任　Class Advisor

辦公室文員　Office Clerk

辦公室主任　Office Administrator

辦公室助理　Office Assistant

部門經理　Branch Manager

保險理賠員　Insurance Claims Controller

保險協調員　Insurance Coordinator

報關員　Customs Clearance Officer

編輯　Editor

播音員　Announcer

簿記員　Bookkeeper

財務報告人　Financial Reporter

財物出納　Treasurer

財務分析員　Financial Analyst

財務經理　Financial Manager

財務主管　Financial Executive

財務總監　Financial Controller

採購部總管　Chief Purchaser

採購員　Buyer / Purchaser / Purchasing Clerk

採購代理　Purchasing Agent

採礦工程師　Mining Engineer

倉儲經理　Warehouse Manager

倉庫主管　Warehouse Supervisor

操作員　Operator

測量工程師　Surveying Engineer

測量員　Surveyor

產科醫生　Obstetrician

產品經理　Product Manager

產品專家　Product Specialist

廠長　Plant / Factory Manager

成本分析員　Costing Analyst

程序設計工程師　Programming Engineer

程序設計經理　Programming Manager

出口部經理　Export Manager

出口業務人員　Export Clerk

出納員　Cashier

初級工程師　Junior Engineer

厨師　Cook
促銷部經理　Sales Promotion Manager
促銷員　Sales Promoter
打字員　Typist
大堂經理　Lobby Manager
大學校長　President
代理校長　Acting President
檔案管理員　Filing Clerk
導遊　Tourist Guide
導演　Director
地區代表　Area Representative
電工　Electrician
電器工程師　Electrical Engineer
電腦操作員　Computer Operator
電腦程序設計員　Programmer
電子工程師　Electronics Engineer
電子技術員　Electronics Technician
店員　Sales Clerk
董事　Director
董事長　Chairman of the Board
兒科醫師　Pediatrician
髮型設計師　Hair-style Designer
法律顧問　Legal Advisor / Legal Consultant
翻譯　Translator
法醫　Judicial Doctor
翻譯審校員　Translation Checker

飯店經理　Restaurant Manager
房地產職員　Real Estate Staff
房地產中介人員 Real Estate Agent / Broker
分公司經理　Branch Manager
副廠長　Assistant Plant Manager
副教授　Associate Professor
副經理　Assistant Manager
副研究員　Associate Researcher
副校長/副總裁　Vice-President
副總工程師　Associate Chief Engineer
副總經理　Deputy General Manager
高級工程師　Senior Engineer
高級顧問　Senior Consultant / Advisor
高級雇員　Senior Employee
高級會計　Senior Accountant
高級經濟師　Senior Economist
高級文案　Senior Copywriter
工程部經理　Engineering Manager
工程技術員　Engineering Technician
工程監理　Engineering Project Supervisor
工程師　Engineer
公共關係經理　Public Relations Manager
管理顧問　Management Consultant
廣告工作人員　Advertising Staff
規劃師　Planner
海關人員　Customs Officer

化學工程師　Chemical Engineer
機械工程師　Mechanical Engineer
計算機操作員　Computer Operator
計算機工程師　Computer Engineer
計算機培訓人員　Computer Training Staff
記者　Correspondent / Reporter
技師　Skilled Technician
技術推銷員　Technical Salesman
技術維修人員　Technical Maintenance Staff
技術員　Technician
家庭教師　Tutor
兼職教授　Part-time Professor
健身教練　Fitness Coach / Trainer
監管員　Supervisor
建築工程師　Architectural Engineer
建築師　Architect
講師　Instructor / Lecturer
校對員　Proofreader
教授　Professor
教務長　Dean / Director of Teaching Affairs
接待員　Receptionist
接線員　Operator
經濟師　Economist
進/出口部經理　Import / Export Manager
酒店經理　Hotel Manager
局域網管理員　LAN Administrator

經銷商　Distributor

客座教授　Guest Professor / Visiting Professor

空中小姐　Air Hostess

口語翻譯　Interpreter

會計（師）　Account

會計部經理　Accounting Manager

快遞員　Courier

律師　Lawyer

面包師　Baker

媒介策劃　Media Planner

美術指導　Art Director

美發師　Hairdresser

名譽教授　Honorary Professor

模特　Model

男/女節目主持人　Host / Hostess

男/女演員　Actor / Actress

品質工程師　Quality Engineer

品質管理檢驗員　QC Inspector

評論員　Commentator

培訓經理/主管　Training Manager / Supervisor

區域經理　District / Regional Manager

人力資源總監　HR Director

人力資源部經理　Human Resources Manager

人事部經理　Personnel Manager

人事部職員　Personnel Clerk

軟件工程師　Software Engineer

設計師　Designer
攝影師　Photographer
審計員　Auditor
生物工程師　Biological Engineer
實習醫生　Intern Doctor
實驗員　Laboratory Technician
實驗室主任　Laboratory Chief
市場策劃人員　Marketing Planner
市場分析員　Market Analyst
市場研究員　Market Researcher
室內裝潢師　Interior Decorator
售貨員　Sales Clerk
私人秘書　Personal / Private Secretary
速記員　Stenographer
調酒師　Alcohol Mixer
同聲傳譯員　Simultaneous Interpreter
統計員　Statistician
投資部經理　Fund Manager
圖書館員　Librarian
土木工程師　Civil Engineer
外科醫生　Surgeon
維修工程師　Maintenance Engineer
文字處理操作員　Wordprocessor Operator
系統操作員　Systems Operator
系統分析員　Systems Analyst
系統工程師　Systems Engineer

項目經理　Project Manager

銷售部經理　Marketing / Sales Manager

銷售代表　Marketing / Sales Representative

銷售監理　Sales Supervisor

銷售員　Salesperson

銷售主管　Market / Sales Executive

銷售助理　Market / Sales Assistant

小學校長　Headmaster

心理醫師　Psychologist

新聞記者　Journalist / Newsman

信用部經理　Credit Manager

信用部職員　Credit Clerk

行政經理　Administration Manager

行政助理　Administration Assistant

行政人員　Administration Staff

學院院長　Dean / Head of College

牙科醫生　Dentist

研發工程師　Research & Development（R & D）Engineer

研究生導師　Research Supervisor

研究員　Researcher

驗票員　Ticket Inspector

藥劑師　Pharmacist

業務經理　Business Manager

醫療技術人員　Medical Technician

音樂教師　Music Teacher

應用工程師　Application Engineer

英語教師　English Instructor / Teacher
硬件工程師　Hardware Engineer
郵政人員　Postal Clerk
宇航員　Astronaut
註册會計師　Certified Public Accountant
製造工程師　Manufacturing Engineer
中學校長　Principle
質量管理工程師　Quality Control Engineer
助教　Teaching Assistant
助理工程師　Assistant Engineer
助理會計師　Assistant Accountant
助理研究員　Assistant Researcher / Research Assistant
專欄作家　Columnist
專業人員　Professional Staff
總編　Chief Editor / Editor in Chief
總裁　President
總工程師　Chief Engineer
總經理　General Manager
總經理秘書　General Manager's Secretary
總經理助理　Assistant to General Manager / General Manager Assistant
總會計師　Chief Accountant
制片人　Producer

第八單元
熱詞、新詞、高頻詞

　　隨著經濟、政治、文化各方面的不斷發展，中國在國際舞臺上扮演了越來越重要的角色，近年來也不斷涌現出衆多的漢語新詞、熱詞，涉及政治類詞彙、法制類詞彙、社會熱點詞彙以及網路流行語等。漢語新詞、熱詞以獨特的方式體現了中國社會的發展和進步，揭示了中國面臨的問題和挑戰，反應着特定時期內人們普遍關注的熱點話題和民生問題，折射出時下廣受關注的焦點、熱點或時尚前沿的流行文化。由於"新詞""熱詞"極具時代特色和文化因素，這類詞彙的翻譯應予以特別重視。

　　本單元介紹近年來漢語裡出現的一些熱詞、新詞以及高頻詞的翻譯，將其大致分爲五類：政治、法治、社會民生、文教以及網路流行語。

一、政治類詞語翻譯

　　十三五規劃（國民經濟和社會發展第十三個五年計劃）　the 13th Five-Year Plan (the 13th Five-Year Plan for Economics and Social

Development of the People's Republic of China）

　　供給側結構性改革　supply-side structural reform

　　改革促進派　reform promoter

　　G20 峰會　G20 summit

　　負面清單管理模式　negative-list management mode

　　工匠精神　spirit of the craftsman

　　新常態　new normal

　　"一帶一路"（絲綢之路經濟帶和 21 世紀海上絲綢之路）　the Belt and Road Initiative（the Silk Road Economic Belt and the 21st Century Maritime Silk Road）

　　權力清單　power lists

　　簡政放權　streamline administrative approvals and delegate power to lower levels

　　高壓態勢　tough stance

　　命運共同體　community with a common future / community of shared destiny

　　絲路基金　Silk Road fund

　　南海仲裁案　the South China Sea Arbitration

　　綜合國力　the overall national strength

　　綠色政治生態體系　green political eco-system

　　政治規矩　political discipline and rules

　　行政監督　administrative supervision

　　政務公開　make government affairs public

　　簡化行政審批程序　streamline administrative examination and approval procedures

　　中華民族偉大復興　great rejuvenation of the Chinese nation

中國精神　Chinese spirit

中國夢　The Chinese dream

中國力量　Chinese strength

美麗中國　beautiful China

第一夫人外交　First Lady diplomacy

新型國際關係　a new kind of international relations

互利共贏的開放戰略　mutually beneficial opening up strategy

中國製造 2025　Made in China 2025 Strategy

獲得感　sense of gain

小康社會　moderately prosperous society

和諧社會　harmonious society

保持戰略定力　maintain strategic focus

穩中求進　make progress while maintaining stability

政治互信　mutual political trust

改革開放　reform and opening up

誠信體系　creditability system

公民道德建設　civic morality construction

中國特色社會主義　socialism with Chinese characteristics

中國特色大國外交理念　the philosophy underpinning China's diplomacy as a major country

社會主義核心價值觀　core socialist values

社會主義榮辱觀　the socialist concept of honor and disgrace

社會主義民主　socialist democracy

社會主義初級階段　primary stage of socialism

社會主義思想道德體系　socialist ideological and ethical system

創新發展　innovative development

協調發展　coordinated development
綠色發展　green development / eco-friendly development
共享發展　shared development
開放發展　open development
引領型發展　leading-edge development
建設創新型國家　to construct an innovative country
精準扶貧和脫貧　take targeted measures to alleviate and eliminate poverty
形象工程　image project
與時俱進　keep up with the times
政治體制改革　political structure reform
政府社會管理職能　government social administration function
人民的根本利益　fundamental interests of the people
以人爲本、執政爲民　always put people first and run the government for the people
世界經濟政治格局　global economic and political patterns
和平共處五項原則　Five Principles of Peaceful Coexistence
和平發展道路　path of peaceful development
求同存異　seek common ground while putting aside differences
祖國和平統一　peaceful reunification of the motherland
兩岸關係和平發展　peaceful development of cross-Straits relations
"一國兩制"　one country, two systems
四項基本原則　The Four Cardinal Principles
特別行政區　Special Administrative Region
民族區域自治　regional ethnic autonomy
科學發展觀　Scientific Outlook on Development

"三個代表"重要思想（代表中國先進生產力的發展要求、代表中國先進文化的發展方向、代表中國最廣大人民的根本利益）
Three Represents (represent the development trend of China's advanced productive forces, the orientation of China's advanced culture and the fundamental interests of the overwhelming majority of the Chinese people)

鄧小平理論　Deng Xiaoping Theory

工作作風　working style

領導核心　core of the leadership

公務員　civil servant

群團組織　mass organization

群眾路線　mass line

黨內民主　intra-Party democracy

國慶閱兵　National Day Military Parade

中國共產黨　the Communist Party of China（CPC）

中央委員會　Central Committee

中央委員　member of the Central Committee

中央委員會總書記　General Secretary of the Central Committee

中央政治局　The Political Bureau of the Central Committee

全國人民代表大會　National People's Congress（NPC）

全國人民代表大會常委會　Standing Committee of the NPC

中國人民政治協商會議　Chinese People's Political Consultative Conference（CPPCC）

政協全國委員會　National Committee of the CPPCC

黨的全國代表大會　The National Congress of the Party

中國共產黨第十八次全國代表大會　The 18th National Congress of the Communist Party of China

中央書記處　Secretariat of the Central Committee

中共中央辦公廳　General Office of the CPC Certral Committee

中國共產主義青年團　the Communist Youth League of China

堅持人民主體地位　uphold the principal position of the people

引領經濟發展新常態　guide the new normal in China's economic development

創新驅動發展戰略　innovation-driven development strategy

發展新動能　new driver of growth

網路強國戰略　national cyber development strategy

構建創新、活力、聯動、包容的世界經濟　build an innovative, invigorated, interconnected and inclusive world economy

遂民意、促發展、利和諧　meet people's will, promote development and facilitate social harmony

"五大發展理念"（創新、協調、綠色、開放、共享）　Five Development Concepts (development of innovation, harmonization, green, openness and sharing)

"三嚴三實"（嚴以修身、嚴以用權、嚴以律己，謀事要實、創業要實、做人要實）　Three Stricts and Three Honests: Be strict in morals, power and disciplining oneself; be honest in decisions, business and behavior)

"四個全面"戰略部署（全面建成小康社會、全面深化改革、全面依法治國、全面從嚴治黨）　Four-Pronged Comprehensive Strategy (comprehensively build a moderately prosperous society; comprehensively deepen reform; comprehensively implement the rule of law; comprehensively strengthen Party discipline)

"兩個一百年"奮鬥目標（在2020年中國共產黨成立一百年時

全面建成小康社會，在2049年新中國成立一百年時建成富強、民主、文明、和諧的社會主義現代化國家） the Two Centenary Goals (The Two Centenary Goals are to finish building a moderately prosperous society in all respects by the time the CPC celebrates its centenary in 2020 and to turn China into a modern socialist country that is prosperous, strong, democratic, culturally advanced, and harmonious by the time the People's Republic of China celebrates its centenary in 2049）

"五位一體"總體布局（全面落實經濟建設、政治建設、文化建設、社會建設、生態文明建設五位一體總體布局） promote all-round economic, political, cultural, social and ecological progress

三期疊加（增長速度換檔期、結構調整陣痛期、前期刺激政策消化期） simultaneously deal with the slowdown in economic growth, make difficult structural adjustments, and absorb the effects of previous economic stimulus policies

深化改革擴大開放 deepen reform and opening up

中高速增長 medium-high rate of economic growth

區域協同發展 coordinated development between regions

眾創、眾包、眾扶、眾籌 popular entrepreneurship, crowd-sourcing, collective support and crowd-funding

人人參與、人人盡力、人人享有 Everyone participates, makes a contribution and shares in the benefits

二、法治類詞語翻譯

反腐倡廉 fight corruption and encourage integrity

對腐敗"零容忍"　zero tolerance for corruption

司法透明　judicial transparency

社會公平正義　social fairness and justice

恪盡職守，廉潔奉公　be committed and honest when performing one's duty

忠誠於憲法，忠實於人民　be true to the Constitution and loyal to the people

行政執法監督　supervision of administrative law enforcement

依法用權，倡儉治奢　exercise power in accordance with the law, encourage thrift and oppose extravagance

黨內監督　intra-Party supervision

反腐監察小組　anti-graft inspection team

憲法宣誓　pledge allegiance to the Constitution

法治政府、創新政府、廉潔政府　law-based, innovative and clean government

尊重並維護憲法和法律的權威　respect and safeguard the authority of the Constitution and laws

規範執法、公正執法、文明執法　enforce laws in a standard, fair and civil manner

中國特色社會主義法律體系　The Socialist System of Laws with Chinese Characteristics

法定職責　obligations given by the laws

行政法規　administrative regulation

社會治安綜合治理　comprehensive maintenance of public order

多元主體共同治理　involve all parties in social governance

人民公僕　servant of the people

合法權益　legitimate rights and interests of citizens

尊重與保護人權　respect and protect human rights

遵紀守法　abide by law and discipline

違法違規行爲　violation of laws and regulations

制度不健全、監管不到位　institutional deficiency and poor oversight

玩忽職守　dereliction of duty

權力過分集中　excessive concentration of power

危害公共安全的犯罪　crime threatening public security

酒後駕駛　drunk driving

網路犯罪　cyber crime

濫用職權　abuse power

以權謀私　abuse power for personal gain

貪污賄賂　corruption and bribery

公車私用　government cars used for private purpose

公費出國出境　use of public funds for traveling abroad

毒品走私　drug smuggling

非法集資　illegal fund-raising

外逃官員　fugitive official

官商勾結　collusion between government officials and business owner

結黨營私、拉幫結派　form cliques to pursue selfish interest

法律程序　legal procedure

拍蠅打虎　crack dawn on the "flies" at the bottom and the "tigers" higher up

掃黃　crackdown on pornography

"追逃"　hunt for those who have fled abroad

舉報網站　tip-off website
"天網"　Sky Net
正當防衛　justifiable defense
政府消費支出　government consumption expenditure
司法體制改革　reform in the judicial system
"三公"消費（政府部門人員因公出國/境經費、公務車購置及運行費、公務招待費產生的消費）　the three public consamptions (official overseas visits, official vehicles and official hospitality)
"四風"（形式主義，官僚主義、享樂主義、奢靡之風）　formalism, bureaucracy, hedonism and extravagance
"雙開"（開除黨籍和開除公職）　expel someone from the CPC and remove someone from public office

三、環保類詞語翻譯

堅持環境保護基本國策　adhere to the basic state policy of environmental protection
資源節約型社會　resource-conserving society
低碳生活方式　low-carbon lifestyle
低碳經濟　low-carbon economy
循環經濟　circular economy
可持續發展　sustainable development
環境保護　environmental protection
環境宜居指數　Environmental Livability Index
氣候變化　climate change

温室效應　greenhouse effect
全球變暖　global warming
環境惡化　environmental deterioration
城市熱島效應　urban heat island effect
空氣質量監測　air quality monitoring
空氣污染濃度　air pollution concentration
空氣污染指數　air pollution index（AQI）
霧霾　haze / smog
橙色預警　orange alert
可吸入顆粒物　inhalable particle
實時發布 PM2.5 數據　release real-time PM2.5 data
健康指標　health indexes
污染物　pollutant
污染源　pollution source
污染源普查　census of pollution sources
有害空氣污染物　hazardous airborne pollutant
防塵口罩　anti-dust gauze mask
沙塵暴　sand storm
二氧化碳排放量　carbon dioxide emissions
溫室氣體排放　greenhouse gas emission
碳減排　carbon emission reduction
能耗　energy consumption
節能減排　energy conservation and emissions reduction
機動車尾氣　vehicle exhaust
工業粉塵排放　industrial dust discharge
工業烟塵　industrial fumes

噪音污染　noise pollution

無車日　Car-Free Day

排污許可證　pollutant discharge license

低耗能汽車　low energy consumption vehicle

尾氣淨化器　exhaust purifier

無鉛汽油　lead-free gasoline

緩解交通阻塞的壓力　relieve the traffic congestion

大功率電器　high-power electrical appliance

能耗　energy consumption

排污費　pollutant discharge fee

大氣監測系統　atmospheric monitoring system

再生資源　renewable resource

資源綜合利用　comprehensive utilization of resources

開發可再生資源　develop renewable resources

環保產品　environment-friendly products

白色污染　white pollution (by using and littering of non-degradable white plastics)

一次性餐具　disposable dishware

一次性餐巾紙　disposable paper tissues

可降解包裝　biodegradable packing

"光盤行動"　clear your plate campaign

污染罰款　pollution fines

世界環境日　World Environment Day (June 5th each year)

森林砍伐率　rate of deforestation

水資源短缺　water shortage

垃圾回收和處理　garbage collection and disposal

城市垃圾　urban garbage

垃圾分類　garbage classification

有限自然資源　limited natural resources

綠色能源　green energy

無污染燃料　pollution-free fuel

太陽能　solar energy

風能　wind energy

清潔能源　clean energy

替代能源　alternative energy

可再生能源　renewable energy

生物能源　bio-energy

核能　nuclear energy

臭氧層　the ozone layer

自然災害　natural disaster

污水治理　sewage treatment

破壞自然栖息地　damage natural habitat

酸雨　acid rain

森林砍伐　deforestation

山體滑坡　landslide

瀕危動物　endangered species

自然保護區　natural reserve

野生動物保護區　wildlife reserve

動物權益保護者　animal rights activist

生態保護紅線　ecological conservation red line

環保技術　environmental technology

生態旅遊　ecotourism

生態城市　eco-city

生態示範區　eco-demonstration region / environment-friendly region

綠化帶　green belt

森林覆蓋率　forest coverage

人工降雨　artificial precipitation

水土保持　conservation of water and soil

全民義務植樹日　National Tree-Planting Day

消防知識教育　fire fighting education

達到防火安全標準　meet fire-proof standards

提高大眾環保意識　raise / arouse people's awareness of environmental protection

四、社會民生類詞語翻譯

漸進式延遲退休年齡　progressively raise retirement age

養老金"並軌"　pension system unification

離退休人員基本養老金　basic pensions for retirees

退休金雙軌制　dual pension scheme

全面兩孩政策　overall second-child policy

二孩經濟　second-child economy

獨生子女政策　one-child policy

空巢老人　empty nester

"低生育陷阱"　low fertility trap

生育率　fertility rate

準生證　birth permissian certificate

慈善法修改　amendment of charity laws

電信詐騙　telecom fraud

二維碼　QR code

微信　WeChat

網路論壇　online forum

光網城市　Cities linked up to fiber-optic networks

互聯網+　Internet plus Initiative

互聯網安全　Internet security

實名註冊　real-name registration

網路打拐行動　online campaign to battle child trafficking

第二代身份證　second-generation ID card

人肉搜索　cyber manhunt

隱私權　privacy right

非法職業介紹機構　illegal job agency

就業歧視　employment discrimination

大學生就業促進計劃　program for promoting employment of university graduates

人力資源市場　human resource market

跳槽　job-hopping

跳槽價值　jump value

選擇焦慮　choice anxiety

全國性房產政策　nationwide property policy

樓市調控　property market regulation

房屋限購　home buying restrictions / property purchase limits

首付　down payment

首次置業者　first-home buyer
按揭貸款　mortgage loan
房產稅　house property tax
廉租房　low-rent house
房屋拆遷　housing demolition
住宅區　residential area
住房公積金　housing accumulation fund
住房租賃市場　home rental market
住房補貼　housing allowances
房地產泡沫　property bubble / real estate bubble
房地產市場　property market
規範房地產中介　regulate real estate agencies
春運　Spring Festival travel rush
黃金周　golden week
雙十一網購節　double 11 online shopping festival
團購　group buying
網購退貨辦法　refund policy for online shopping
購買力　purchasing power
超前消費　excessive consumption
節後綜合徵　after-holiday syndrome
一線城市　first-tier city
食品安全　food safety
非法食品添加劑　illegal food additives
轉基因食品　genetically modified (gm) food
食品藥品安全　food and drug safety
人民生活水平　people's living standard

保障民生 protection of people's livelihood
勞動合同制度 labor contract system
社會救助體系 social assistance system
帶薪休假制度 system of paid vacations
縮小收入差距 narrow the income gap
城鄉發展一體化 urban-rural integration
社會保障基金 social security fund
中國特色城鎮化 urbanization with Chinese characteristics
城鎮社會保障體系 urban social security system
下崗職工基本生活費 subsistence allowances for laid-off workers
醫保制度改革 reform of medical insurance system
醫患關係 relation between doctors and patients
醫患糾紛 patient-doctor disputes / medical disputes
整形手術 plastic surgery
器官捐獻 organ donation
器官移植手術 organ transplant surgery
抗生素濫用 overuse of antibiotics
個人信用記錄 personal credit record
信用評級體系 credit rating system
亞健康 sub-health
重大疾病保險（重疾險） critical illness insurance program
生育險 maternity insurance
人壽險 life insurance
醫療、醫保、醫藥聯動改革 coordinated healthcare, health insurance, and pharmaceutical reforms
機關事業單位養老保險制度改革 reform of the pension system for

government and public institution employees
　　　績效工資　performance-based salary
　　　高溫補貼　high-temperature subsidies
　　　加班費　overtime pay
　　　嚴厲打擊非法用工　severely punish illegal employment
　　　廉價勞動力　cheap labor force
　　　勞動合同法　labor contract law
　　　就業機會　employment opportunities
　　　失業保險制度　unemployment insurance system
　　　"零就業"家庭　zero-employment family
　　　鼓勵自謀職業和自主創業　encourage people to find jobs on their own or start their own businesses
　　　公共就業服務體系　public employment service system
　　　落實促進殘疾人就業政策　carry out policies to find more jobs for people with physical and mental disabilities
　　　正能量　positive energy
　　　婦女權益　women's rights and interests
　　　家暴　family / domestic violence
　　　留守兒童　left-behind children
　　　戶籍制度　household registration system
　　　戶口遷移政策　household registration transfer policy
　　　農民工市民化　urbanization of migrant workers
　　　婚前協議　prenuptial agreement
　　　婚前同居　cohabitation before marriage
　　　婚前體檢　pre-marriage medical check-up
　　　試管嬰兒　test-tube baby

代孕媽媽　surrogate mother
脫貧攻堅工程　poverty alleviation program
收入分配　income distribution
低收入群眾　low-income people
弱勢群體　disadvantaged groups
農民工　migrant worker
貧困線　poverty line
收入差距　income gap
勞動力過剩/短缺　labor surplus / shortage
非法收入　illegal income
經營許可證　business certificate
福利彩票　welfare lottery
汽車購買配額　vehicle purchase quotas
牌照單雙號限行措施　odd-even license plate system
公車卡　public transport card
衛星定位裝置　GPS device
電商平臺　e-commerce platform
叫車軟件　car-hailing apps
拼車　carpooling / car sharing
"優步化"　uberization
黑計程　unlicensed taxi
計程車起步價　starting taxi fare
不公平競爭　unfair competition
計程車行業改革　reforms in taxi industry
大眾旅遊時代　new era of mass tourism
跟團旅遊　package tour

深度遊　in-depth travel
自駕遊　self-driving tour
旅遊簽證　tourist visa
落地簽　visa on arrival
不文明行爲　inappropriate / uncivilized behavior
72 小時過境免簽　72-hour visa-free transit
單次／多次入境簽證　single / multiple entry visa
世界愛滋病日　World AIDS Day
愛滋病病毒携帶者　HIV carriers
真人秀　reality show / reality TV
電視真人秀明星　reality TV star
廣場舞　guangchangwu / public square dancing
公共服務設施　public service facilities
基礎設施建設　infrastructure construction

五、文教類詞語翻譯

科教興國戰略　strategy of reinvigorating China through science and education
人才強國戰略　strategy of reinvigorating China through human resource development
國家文化軟實力　China's cultural soft power
《國家中長期人才發展規劃綱要》China's Medium and Long-term Talent Development Plan
教育扶貧工程　project to alleviate poverty through education

優化教育結構　optimize the education structure
非物質文化遺產　intangible cultural heritage
信息共享平臺　information-sharing platform
知識產權　intellectual property right
人文交流　cultural and people-to-people exchange
選人用人制度　system for selecting and employing personnel
"千人計劃"　1 000 Talents Plan / Thousand Talents Program
引進人才　to bring in talents
大科學工程　Big Science Project
國家公務員考試　national civil servant examination
翻轉課堂（翻轉教學）　flipped classroom（flip teaching）
慕課（大規模在線開放課程）　Massive Open Online Courses（MOOC）
微課　micro-lecture
招生體制　enrollment system
彈性學制　flexible educational system
招生詐騙　enrollment scam
防作弊舉措　anti-cheating measure
校園招聘會　on-campus job fair
網路主權　internet sovereignty
網路侵權　internet copyright infringement
商標侵權　trademark infringement
盜版軟件　pirated software
教育資源分配不均　uneven distribution of educational resources
同等教育機會　equal opportunity for education
心理健康干預　mental health intervention

戒毒康復中心　drug rehabilitation center
新興媒體　emerging media
高科技領域　high-tech fields
科技創新　scientific and technological innovation
專利產品　patented product
註冊商標　registered trademark
人工智能應用　artificial intelligence application
山寨應用　fake app
電子競技　e-sports
自助圖書館　self-service library
高校擴招計劃　college expansion plan
爭搶生源　poaching of talented students
學雜費　tuition and fees
高校學費上漲　college tuition increase
免學費　tuition waivers
國家助學貸款　national student loan
高考　National College Entrance Examination（NCEE）
"高考移民"　NCEE migrant
高考加分政策　preferential policy that awards bonus points in the National College Entrance Examination
高考狀元　Gaokao top scorer
考生　examinee / exam-taker / candidate
準考證　exam attendance docket
錄取通知書　admission / acceptance letter
"減負"　alleviate academic burden / reduce（ease）academic burden

學生手冊　student guidebook
研究生入學考試　post-graduate entrance examination
公費研究生　government-supported graduate student
自費研究生　self-supporting graduate student
學分制　credit system
校車安全　school bus safety
校園欺凌　school bullying
學術評價體系　academic appraisal system
學術欺詐　academic fraud
學術誠信　academic integrity
學術論文　academic paper
科研經費　research funds
教師輪崗制度　teacher swap system
教師終身制　teacher tenure
師德　teachers' code of morality
教育差距　educational gap
文化逆差　cultural deficit
文化滲透　cultural immersion
素質教育　quality-oriented education
應試教育　exam-oriented education
義務教育　compulsory education
繼續教育　continuing education
現代遠程教育　modern distance education
電影分級制度　film rating system
英語能力測評體系　English proficiency testing and rating system

六、網路流行語翻譯

輕奢品　Entry lux / entry luxe
盲目點讚黨　blind liker
吐槽　make complaints
標題黨　sensational headline writer
搏出位　seek attention
"段子手"　punster（people who are good at making jokes, especially on social media）
"吃瓜群眾"　people who are kept in the dark / spectators / onlookers
"萌萌噠"　adorable / cute / lovely
"賣萌"　act / play cute
"網紅"　Internet celebrity
"呆萌"　adorkable（dorky+ adorable）
"低頭族"　phubbers
"腦殘粉"　fanboy / fangirl
心塞　feel stifled
辣妹　spice girl
蘿莉　lolita / lovely little girl
"洪荒之力"　prehistorical powers / mystic energy
忘年戀　May-December romance
社交控　FOMO addiction（FOMO：fear of missing out）
"智能手機眼盲症"　smartphone blindness

在家啃老的"奇葩族"　"kippers"（kids in parents' pockets eroding retirement savings）

鄰家女孩　girl next door

情感垃圾桶　emotional trashcan

小窗口私聊　side-text

自拍　selfie

情侶自拍　couplie

肥皂劇　soap opera

土豪生活　jet setting lifestyle

密集恐懼症　trypophobia

"備胎"　rebound guy／girl

"資訊癖"　infomania

加好友　Friending

辦公室八卦　watercooler games

朋友圈行銷　friendvertising

網路遊民　Internet hobo

"女漢子"　tough girl／manly woman

"軟妹子"　girly girl

經濟適用女／男　budget wife／husband

宅女　home-bound girl／shut-in girl／house girl

正妹　hotty／beautiful girl

"白骨精"　female office elite

"虎媽"　tiger mother

乖乖女　well-behaved girl／obedient girl

"剩男剩女"　left-over men and women

"僵屍車"　zombie cars

"必剩客"　doomed single
海歸　overseas returnee
"秒殺"　seckill / speed kill
淡定　calm / unruffled
腹黑　scheming
悲催　a tear-inducing misery
"黃金單身族"　golden single
表情圖標　emoji
QQ 表情　QQ emoji
網遊　online game
表情智商　emoji IQ
我也是"醉了"　I'm speechless / Are you kidding me?
感覺身體被掏空　I am worn-out / I am dog-tired
嚇死"本寶寶"了　I'm scared to death

參考文獻

[1] 北京外國語學院英語系. 新編漢英分類詞彙手冊 [M]. 北京：外語教學與研究出版社，1983.

[2] 陳紅薇，李亞丹. 新編漢英翻譯教程 [M]. 上海：上海外語教育出版社，2004.

[3] 馮修文，李柯. 中國古典詩詞中的傳統文化（英文版）[M]. 上海：上海交通大學出版社，2015.

[4] 梁爲祥，肖輝，陶長安. 新詞，流行詞，常用詞翻譯 [M]. 南京：東南大學出版社，2014.

[5] 尚春瑞. 如何書寫英文簡歷 [M]. 天津：天津科技翻譯出版公司，2006.

[6] 上海市語言文字工作委員會辦公室，上海市公共場所名稱英譯專家委員會秘書處. 公共場所英語標識語錯譯解析與規範 [M]. 上海：上海外語教育出版社，2010.

[7] 司顯柱，趙海燕. 漢譯英教程新編 [M]. 上海：東華大學出版社，2012.

[8] 吳光華. 漢英大辭典 [M]. 上海：上海譯文出版社，2009.

[9] 楊永林. 常用標誌英文譯法手冊 [M]. 北京：商務印書館，

2012.

［10］張白樺. 趣味英漢互譯教程［M］. 北京：清華大學出版社，2015.

［11］http：//baike. so. com.

［12］http：//english. cri. cn.

［13］http：//english. peopledaily. com. cn.

［14］http：//en. wikipedia. org.

［15］http：//gxedu. org. cn.

［16］http：//language. chinadaily. com. cn.

［17］http：//scenery. nihaowang. com.

［18］http：//studyabroad. tigtag. com.

［19］http：//www. chinadaily. com. cn.

［20］http：//www. hjenglish. com.

［21］http：//www. i21st. cn.

［22］http：//www. 51yala. com.

國家圖書館出版品預行編目(CIP)資料

實用大學英語翻譯手冊 / 朱豔、王宏宇 主編. -- 第一版.
-- 臺北市：崧燁文化，2018.08
　面；　公分

ISBN 978-957-681-392-4(平裝)

1.英語教學 2.高等教育

805.103　　　　　　107011666

書　名：實用大學英語翻譯手冊
作　者：朱豔、王宏宇 主編
發行人：黃振庭
出版者：崧燁文化事業有限公司
發行者：崧燁文化事業有限公司
E-mail：sonbookservice@gmail.com
粉絲頁　　　　　　網　址：
地　址：台北市中正區重慶南路一段六十一號八樓 815 室
8F.-815, No.61, Sec. 1, Chongqing S. Rd., Zhongzheng Dist., Taipei City 100, Taiwan (R.O.C.)
電　話：(02)2370-3310　傳　真：(02) 2370-3210
總經銷：紅螞蟻圖書有限公司
地　址：台北市內湖區舊宗路二段 121 巷 19 號
電　話：02-2795-3656　傳　真：02-2795-4100　網址：
印　刷：京峯彩色印刷有限公司（京峰數位）

　　本書版權為西南財經大學出版社所有授權崧博出版事業股份有限公司獨家發行電子書繁體字版。若有其他相關權利需授權請與西南財經大學出版社聯繫，經本公司授權後方得行使相關權利。

定價：400 元

發行日期：2018 年 8 月第一版

◎ 本書以POD印製發行